Jessica tr_
to scramble off the bed

Matt grinned as he stretched out beside her. "Was it pure luck that you chose to come to my bed tonight or was it strictly for Kristin's benefit?"

"I knew she was plotting something," she said sharply, disturbed by the powerful length of him. "I heard her sneaking around. I had to act quickly."

"And instinctively, hmm?" His hand brushed her cheek. "You didn't have to come and get in my bed, though. You could have pretended a nightmare, screamed 'fire' or used any number of clever devices. You can't tell me it was all for Kristin— you knew how I'd react. It's like getting an engraved invitation to make love to you."

"No, Matt," she said weakly, knowing the truth of every word.

"Yes, Jess—" He lowered his mouth to hers. . . .

SUSAN NAPIER was born on Valentine's Day, so perhaps it is only fitting that she should become a romance writer. She started out as a reporter for New Zealand's largest evening newspaper before resigning to marry the paper's chief reporter. After the birth of their two children she did some free-lancing for a film production company and then settled down to write her first romance. "Now," she says, "I am in the enviable position of being able to build my career around my home and family."

Books by Susan Napier

HARLEQUIN PRESENTS
885—SWEET AS MY REVENGE

HARLEQUIN ROMANCE
2711—LOVE IN THE VALLEY
2723—SWEET VIXEN

These books may be available at your local bookseller.

Don't miss any of our special offers. Write to us at the following address for information on our newest releases.

Harlequin Reader Service
901 Fuhrmann Blvd., P.O. Box 1397, Buffalo, NY 14240
Canadian address: P.O. Box 2800, Postal Station A,
5170 Yonge St., Willowdale, Ont. M2N 6J3

SUSAN NAPIER

sweet as my revenge

Harlequin Books

TORONTO • NEW YORK • LONDON
AMSTERDAM • PARIS • SYDNEY • HAMBURG
STOCKHOLM • ATHENS • TOKYO • MILAN

For my friend,
Anne Donaldson

Harlequin Presents first edition May 1986
ISBN 0-373-10885-0

Original hardcover edition published in 1985
by Mills & Boon Limited

CHAPTER ONE

CLOUDS scudded across a sickly moon. It was a brief but welcome cover for the furtive figure heaving itself up the side of a high granite wall with the help of a stout rope anchored in place by a lethal-looking grappling hook.

The breeze stiffened and again the disinterested face of the moon appeared. In its cold, wan light the figure could now be seen clinging precariously to the rolling coils of barbed wire which ran along the narrow top of the wall. Crouching, covered from head to foot in dark clothing, it looked barely human. The figure moved, flexing strangely lumpy limbs. A long, low, penetrating whistle issued from the small mouth-slit of the all-concealing black balaclava.

Head cocked, the figure listened. When there was no response the whistle sounded again, lingering on the chilly night air. There was a faint, harsh noise in the distance and the figure tensed, gripping the wire more tightly than ever.

The noise became a tearing, then a crashing, in the undergrowth that screened the inner circumference of the wall. Suddenly two lean and lethal Doberman pinschers exploded through the bushes, barking ferociously as they spied their quarry, razor teeth slashing the darkness as they threw themselves in a futile frenzy against the eight-foot wall.

The black-clad figure whistled one last time, taunting the dogs to new heights of fury. An arm moved in a rapid, arcing motion. A soft thump came from the undergrowth behind the animals, sending them slavering after the scent. For half a minute they moved back and forth indecisively, barking at the unreachable figure on the wall and returning to sniff and whine among the long, spiky grasses.

Finally they succumbed to temptation, starting to tear at what *was* reachable, still dancing with tense excitement, keeping the silent watcher in sight, lifting their heads alternately to emit savage warning growls.

Having finished eating they began to bark again, but with less enthusiasm and eventually they quietened completely, staggering in circles and sinking to the ground with short, bewildered whines.

With a quiet laugh the figure on the wall launched into the air, landing beside the supine dogs with a practised, rolling fall that harmlessly absorbed the shock of the hard earth. Rising tall, the figure displayed a solid, chunky build, with a breadth of shoulder that reinforced the overall impression of fitness and strength.

Passing the dogs without another glance the intruder pushed through the bushes to pause at the edge of a wide, undulating lawn. From its centre rose a great, shadowy manor house, dominating the landscape with gothic ugliness. There were a few ancient oaks studding the manicured lawn, but precious little else to use as cover. The broad shoulders rose and fell as the figure in the shadows took a series of deep, rapid breaths, before setting off in a fast, loping run towards the house.

Muffled feet made barely a sound on the raked gravel as the intruder rounded the front corner of the manor, keeping close to the stone walls, moving rapidly yet with caution.

The blind stone lions guarding the solid oak door ignored the shadow that flitted past them and fumbled briefly with the ultra-modern steel lock that marred the antique perfection of the oak panels. The key glinted briefly as it was withdrawn, then the door yielded silently, opening inwards on to a flagstoned hall.

Swiftly the intruder stepped inside, pulling the door closed and pausing for a few precious seconds, adjusting to the inky blackness. Moving again now, down the hall with confident tread, to another firmly closed door which yielded to another key.

With an audible sigh the nocturnal visitor leaned against the panelled door surveying the gloomy room. Here the darkness was less solid, the small lead-light windows permitting the gliding of a grudging moon. After a brief tour of the desk and antique display cabinets the figure stood before the shadowy outline of a bookcase. One black-gloved hand fumbled along the third row of books and pulled out the seventh, a heavy tome bound in leather. Reaching into the narrow rectangular recess left by the removal of the book, the figure succeeded in producing a quiet, satisfying click. Suddenly part of the upper portion of the bookcase slid back to reveal the smug, steely-grey face of a sophisticated modern safe.

The figure stepped back into the centre of the room, and there was a soft rustling. Trousers, sweater and balaclava fell to the carpet in a patch of moonshine that was quickly doused as the thick velvet curtains were pulled across the window.

The total darkness lasted only a moment. There was another gentle click and the desk-lamp flared to life. The chunky intruder was gone. Instead, there stood a tall, lithe young woman, exquisitely coiffured and made-up, dressed in a full-length black evening gown, her ears and throat ablaze with diamonds and rubies!

CHAPTER TWO

JESSICA WRIGHT shook out the fine jersey of her evening gown.

'Thank God for the miracle of modern fabrics,' she murmured as she deftly rolled up her discarded clothing into a grapefruit-sized ball and stuffed them into her black shoulder bag.

She straightened and took a deep breath, spreading her hands and holding them up in front of her face. Steady as a rock. A smile widened her already generously wide mouth. She had never expected to feel like this ... exhilarated, alive, the sharp edge of fear adding to, rather than detracting from, her excitement. Perhaps she should take up cat burglary for a living!

She turned to check her appearance in the reflective glass front of a display case. Mmmm ... every inch a society lady, dressed for a carefree night on the town. The diamonds were paste, but no one was going to get close enough to realise it ...

The black gown had been chosen mostly for its uncanny ability to retain its shape after almost any mistreatment, but also for its value as a distraction. The sleeves were short, the shoulders discreetly padded, the wrap-over neck slightly loose, pouching softly as it plunged to the artificial red rose tucked in the silver belt at her waist. Jessica was a tall woman, with a physique to match and the dress displayed a good deal of what she had. The wide expanse of skin glowed with a healthy tan, broken here and there by strategic clusters of freckles. Her face was classically oval, but not classically beautiful—striking she had been called on more than one occasion, not necessarily as a compliment. She suspected that her size, her strength and unassailable self-confidence held a strong attraction for men at the same time as it made them wary and uncomfortable. Jessica smoothed back the light brown hair which fell in thick, natural waves to her squared shoulders. Her brown eyes glinted with scorn. In her opinion it was *man* who was the weaker sex, conditioned as he was by centuries of dominance into taking female subordination for granted. Now that the balance was being redressed he howled 'foul', dismayed by the qualities in women that were so admired in men: determination to succeed; belief in oneself; willingness to take risks; sexual freedom ... which for a woman could mean the right to say *no* and not feel guilty about it.

Jessica gave herself one last look. Who, seeing her now, would guess the truth? That she was not a rich society lady, but a middle-class nobody from New Zealand, in a strange country, in a strange house, intent on theft. Therein lay the beauty of her plan!

She checked her watch. Too late to get cold feet. She had come this far ... time to get on with the job.

She looked at the painting on the wall behind the desk—so far all the information she had been given had been spot-on. The brandy decanter was there too, on the table by the window, and she poured a generous measure into one of the crystal balloon glasses beside it. She put the glass down on the desk and tugged the black evening gloves higher up to her elbows as she crossed to the safe.

She flexed her fingers before she touched the double combination dials ... safecrackers always did that in the movies. Not that she needed to; technically she wasn't cracking the safe at all. She repeated the numbers softly to herself as she slowly turned the dials and in less than a minute the heavy safe door swung silently open.

Jessica studied the two shelves. The top one contained a number of boxes, stamped with the discreet initials of famous jewellery houses. Jessica ignored them. Carefully she withdrew the stack of papers from the lower shelf and sought what she had come for.

There. She gripped the bundle of envelopes held together with a rubber band. Quickly she counted them. Good, all there. She put the rest of the papers back into the safe and knelt on the floor, pulling off the rubber band and spreading the envelopes out on the carpet, in order of their post marks.

Reaching into her evening bag she pulled out some folded sheets of paper and with rapid efficiency began extracting the contents of the envelopes and replacing them with the sheets from her bag, checking each one carefully to ensure that the dates at the top of the pages matched the post marks on the envelopes.

The whole process only took five minutes and Jessica was amused by her own unflustered calm. Why, there was nothing to this crime business. Providing you approached it with commonsense, planned well ahead and allowed for contingencies, you had it made. Of course, the inside help was almost a guarantee of success. The real danger was coping with the heady excitement that the illicit promotes. All that adrenalin pumping through your veins, urging you on, daring you. She wished she could be a fly on the wall when *this* crime was discovered . . . which wouldn't be for weeks yet.

Jessica restacked the envelopes and secured them with the rubber band, replacing them in the safe exactly as they had been. As she swung the safe shut and twirled the dials she breathed a hefty sigh, suddenly conscious of the tension at the back of her neck. The strain was there, even though it had been smothered by the allure of danger until now.

She gathered up the discarded bundle of papers from the floor and stared at them grimly. All this trouble, all this heartache and desperation, over a few pieces of paper.

She checked the cold grate of the stone fireplace. The English spring had come late this year, and there were some ashes there, swept to the back but enough for her purpose. She crushed each sheet in her hand into an individual, loose ball, carefully avoiding the blue handwriting that leapt out to catch her eye. It's a wonder I have to do this at all, she thought wryly, from all accounts the words should have ignited the paper themselves.

She lit the little pile with the crystal cigarette lighter from the mantle and watched as the papers burned blue and red and curled into ash. This was using up vital minutes but she had no intention of getting caught with incriminating evidence. That was the whole point of this risky exercise. Providing she hadn't actually broken and entered, providing there was no proof of intention to commit burglary, then the laws of England would protect her. If arrested she could only be charged with trespass.

There, Carl, it's done. Jessica stirred the ashes with the solid brass poker that hung at the fireside, then she tidily brushed the ashes into the older, grey pile, in the grate and mixed them up.

She rose gracefully from the hearth, dusting off her gloves. Mission impossible accomplished. She looked around, checking for any clues she may have inadvertently left behind. The brandy glass!

Jessica picked it up. Should she pour it back? Did the butler check the levels to make sure that no one was nicking the boss's Napoleon? Or should she knock it back herself? Drive off the chills that were beginning to feather her skin. That insidious tension was beginning to tell as her earlier euphoria faded.

'Can I help you ... or are you just browsing?'

Jessica gasped and swung violently around, spilling brandy from the narrow mouth of the glass as she stared, eyes rounded in horror at the open door behind her. Too late she remembered that she should have locked the door again when she came through. Oh, God, was this the end? The annihilation of all their plans? She tried to stave off panic as she stared at the apparition in the doorway.

He stood, arms akimbo, completely blocking her escape route. Jessica had never seen him before in her life but she knew instantly who he was ... that confident sarcasm allied to a faint Australian burr said it all.

So this was Matthew Grieve. The black-hearted villain whose ace card she had just burned in his very own grate; the sadistic money-machine who was supposed to be in Tokyo at this very moment, adding yet another million to his already indecently swollen coffers. Jessica's palms began to sweat.

He didn't look so villainous, she persuaded herself nervously ... not dressed as he was in a short, brown silk kimono and apparently little else. He didn't even look particularly dangerous, the faint menace he was directing towards her muted by obvious exhaustion. He looked as if he had just crawled out of a deep, drugging, unsatisfying sleep. His dark brown, collar-length hair was matted, his dark brown eyes puffy beneath straight brows, and sunken into the narrow skull. He wasn't even very tall, thought Jessica, who had invested his image with the stature of an ogre. Only an inch or so taller than her own five foot ten, and not as fit-looking as she had expected a merciless avenger to be ... not even any hair on his chest!

Jessica's badly shaken confidence began to return.

Probably his reputation was highly over-rated; he looked decidedly unsavoury, but rather weak. All that money and fast living was bound to have a degenerative effect on physical and mental health. Why, the man was swaying on his feet! Drunk, or hung-over, or both. Jessica found her voice, made it fluttery and feminine.

'Goodness, you gave me a fright!' She smoothed her damp palms down the side of her dress in a vaguely provocative movement. 'I thought you were the ghost of the headless knight, come to lure me to my death. John told me the place was haunted. Are you one of his colleagues?'

'John?' The dark eyes remained steady on her face, but with a slightly de-focused look that further increased Jessica's confidence.

'John. Monks.' She smiled nicely. Never say more than you have to ... she had learned that from watching crime shows too.

'John's at a wedding in Taunton; overnight.' Suspicion began to gather as his eyes cleared. So far her appearance had prevented him from immediately assuming she was a burglar. Now she would have to go into her well rehearsed routine.

'We *were* at the wedding. We got bored.' She shrugged smilingly, inviting him to share the joke. As this man's domestic secretary John Monks must be an efficient worker to survive in the job, but it was well-known that he was a womaniser, in spite of being on the wrong side of fifty. Jessica's information was that he favoured young girls of the 'dissolute deb' type. At twenty-six Jessica had her doubts as to whether she fitted into the category of young girl, but she could play the other role as well as the next desperate woman. She moistened her lips and smiled again. 'John brought me home for a few drinks.'

'In *my* office?' His eyes narrowed on her smile. If

everything else about him was brown, his voice wasn't. It was pure blue ice. He was angry and his eyes went over her revealing dress with bleary contempt. But her ploy had been successful, his anger was directed at the insubordination of an employee, rather than at her.

'Oh!' Jessica gave a convincing gasp, setting down the brandy glass and fluttering coyly at him. '*You're* Matthew Grieve? I'm sorry, I didn't recognise you. John told me you were away.' She laughed huskily and increased her smile a notch. She was beginning to enjoy herself, adrenalin racing anew. There was an intense satisfaction in confounding the source of her recent worries. 'I'm sorry for invading your private domain like this, but John told me about your Turner and I was just *dying* to see it. He's my *favourite* artist. I so *envy* you having one of his *gorgeous* paintings.' She waved at the canvas on the wall behind the desk. Nervously, afraid she might have overdone the gushing, she added: 'John thought you wouldn't mind if I had a tiny peek before we——' She put a hand over her mouth and looked at him through lowered lashes.

'Where is he now?' he asked, in a tone that gave nothing away, though his face wore a cynically knowing expression.

'He's not going to get into trouble, is he, for bringing me here?' Jessica asked, taking a step towards him. She had to get closer if she was to carry out her rapidly amended plan. All the while she was watching, simpering, giving an impression of complete vapidness, her clever brain was sorting the options. She couldn't fail now, not when she was so very near to success.

Alert as she was, she saw the slight signs of renewed suspicion, the tensing of his shoulders, the lift of the narrow jaw. He had stopped swaying, his own sluggish brain working. Any moment now he was going to realise that something was wrong.

Jessica lifted a casual hand and fingered the

diamond collar that hugged her throat, moving her head so that the rubies in her drop-earrings caught the light.

It worked like a charm. What thief would come to work dressed so impractically ... decked out in thousands of pounds worth of jewellery? Jessica could see his mind working. His body fell back into weary lines and she took another step towards him, swinging her hips with aplomb.

'I wouldn't like to cause trouble,' she husked. 'After all, I was the one who asked if I could see the house. I know he should have asked permission but he thought you were away. I'm the one you should be angry with. Is there anything I can say ...' another step '... or do, to get you to forgive me?'

He watched her approach with cynical curiosity, eyes sinking heavily once more to the deep inverted triangle of tanned flesh at her front. Jessica got the unpleasant feeling that this wasn't the first time another man's woman had flashed him the come-on. She willed him to respond at the same time as she prepared herself to despise him for doing so.

'What would you suggest?' His mouth barely moved with the words, as if he was too tired even to articulate. His libido must be permanently set on automatic, functioning even when he was practically unconscious!

'Well ...' Jessica moved so that her body was only inches away from his and gave him a first-degree smoulder. 'Well ... I suppose ...' She swayed towards him, enveloping him in a cloud of *Madame Rochas*. 'I suppose ...' She slid her arms up around his warm neck. 'I could ...' She didn't have to go up on her toes, just lean her face into his. His mouth was warm, tasting faintly of whisky and cigars, and totally unresponsive.

Jessica pulled her head away and pouted, eyes as

slumberous as she could make them. 'Perhaps if you
can find something urgent for John to see to, I can
show you exactly what I could do,' she murmured
huskily, hiding her frustration at this bland reaction to
her blatancy. The man must be made of stone, either
that or her charms were slipping.

She leaned forward again and kissed the corner of
his down-turned mouth, pressing her almost bared
breasts against his chest. Warm skin met warm skin
and Jessica shivered at the intimacy of the contact. She
insinuated her hips against his and found to her
intense confusion that he definitely *wasn't* wearing
anything under the kimono, and that in spite of his
blandness, he *was* affected by her actions. Instead of
being softly slack from over-indulgence, the body she
was pressing herself against was taut and hard.

At that moment he confirmed her discovery by
catching the tongue that feathered his lips between his
teeth and biting it gently but firmly. Jessica felt a
sharp jolt of awareness and gasped against his mouth
as one of his hands slid inside her loose gown and
cupped her naked breast.

'No——!' she arched away slightly but although his
head drew back, his hand stayed firmly in position,
fingers stroking deliberately over the silky swell.

'No? Did I misunderstand the message?' His dark
eyes mocked her with the absurdity of her sudden
withdrawal.

'Of course not!' she averred, furious at the way he
had reversed the advantage. Her breast seemed to
throb beneath his hand, heat radiating out over her
chest, tightening the muscles in her throat so that it
was an effort to speak. Angrily she kissed him again,
trying to retrieve the position. It was one of her best
knock-'em-for-a-six kisses, just the right combination
of passion and aggression that experience had taught
her intimidated most men. Only, to her dismay, it

didn't intimidate this man. If anything he seemed more aroused, and Jessica became more desperate.

'What about John?' she attempted, twisting her shoulders to try and dislodge the intrusive hand. To her relief he let his arm fall, with a last stroking flick of his fingers that left her nipples clearly outlined against her dress.

'John?' he murmured, studying her flushed and nervous face.

Now. Here was her chance, while his mind and body were affected by the conflicting demands of sleep and sex.

With a gliding movement Jessica moved back so that her feet were apart, knees slightly bent and whole body relaxed. She smiled, and as his mouth twitched cynically in return she made her move, stepping in, grasping his loose robe at his lapel and sleeve, turning in as she moved. With a neat, rapid movement she broke his balance and executed a perfect Floating Hip Throw. She heard his exclamation as he fell, felt his body go limp in self-defence. Normally she would have assisted his fall so that he didn't hurt himself, but this wasn't a friendly judo bout. Besides, he deserved it for being such a swine, and for making her feel— even if it was only for a few timeless moments— helplessly excited by the way he had kissed and touched her.

An instant later, all satisfaction at her revenge had fled. Jessica stared in horror at the still figure at her feet. My God, she had killed him!

She sank shakily to her knees beside him, stripping off a glove to pull back his limp eyelids. Perhaps he was faking? But no, he was genuinely unconscious. Heart attack? She touched his smooth chest, felt the slow, steady beat and felt her own heartbeat slow. Then what . . .?

She ran her hand through the thick, silky brown

hair. There! A distinct lump . . . though no blood. He
had curled up his body as he fell, but in flipping him
over her hip she had spun closer to one of the display
cabinets. His head must have clipped one of the
ornately carved feet as he landed . . . her mind had
vaguely registered the faint rattle that must have been
the vibration of the porcelain on the glass shelves.

Jessica sat back on her heels feeling sick. How could
something that started out so well end so disastrously?
Theft could be condoned, if—as with Jessica—it was a
matter of righting a wrong. But murder was another
thing entirely!

What should she do? Call for an ambulance? Her
eyes fell on the grate. If there were only herself to
think of she would do just that. But there was Carl . . .
and others. But to go now, and leave him lying
unconscious was unthinkable. What if he died, or was
permanently injured?

She ran over to the desk and picked up the brandy.
Perhaps the smell would revive him . . . she didn't
dare try to get him to drink it . . . he might choke.

There was no response. A frightening thought
occurred to her. If Matthew Grieve was home
unexpectedly there could be others! She looked at her
watch. No time for debate.

She got to her feet, leaving the glass beside the
prone body. He might need it when he recovered. *If*
he recovered. She shouldered the thought aside. She
would go, and when she was safely away she would
ring up. If there was no answer she'd call an
ambulance. That meant police. Damn, damn!

Quelling her screaming conscience, Jessica grabbed
her bag and ran. At the door she hesitated, taking one
last look at her helpless victim. He looked almost
boyish lying there, cleansed of cynicism and dissipation
by unconsciousness. *I'm sorry*, Jessica apologised to
the blameless boy. On impulse she plucked the rose

from her waist and tossed it over to land beside the brandy glass, hoping he would understand the tacit message.

As she fled the silent house, Jessica cursed unruly fate. Now there was a witness, there would be an investigation. If those altered letters were discovered . . .! But perhaps Matthew Grieve wouldn't call in the police. What man likes to admit he was bested by a woman . . . and so easily? If he found nothing missing, might he not assume he had interrupted her before she managed to steal anything?

On the other hand Matthew Grieve was a man who gave no quarter to his enemies. Carl was proof of that. Now Jessica Wright was numbered among them. Thank God there was nothing to connect her with Carl. In two days time she would be safely back in New Zealand. Matthew Grieve might have perfected the art of revenge, but he wasn't omniscient. If he didn't know who she was, he couldn't touch her.

She hadn't bothered to put her concealing clothing back on. This time she left by the gate, easily climbing the wrought iron barrier by hitching up her full skirt. She ran lightly in her black ballet shoes to the place where she had hidden the dark-coloured hire car under some overhanging trees at the side of the road.

Jessica forced herself to drive away without a backward glance. She must get to a telephone as soon as possible. But her first loyalty was still to Carl. First she must put him out of his misery.

CHAPTER THREE

JESSICA'S heart slammed against her chest. Her hands on the wheel were trembling with fear, her mouth dry. She couldn't believe that she had actually done it: robbery with violence! She was a respectable businesswoman, for God's sake, with a reputation for being honest, hard-working and responsible.

She groaned. She had certainly shredded that reputation tonight. She must have been insane to risk it. What if she hadn't known judo? She'd be back there still, compromising herself even further with that awful man. Awful, *unconscious* man! She gave a half-sob, jamming her foot down on the accelerator.

Around every concealed corner she expected to run the gauntlet of police cars. At home the country roads were often as narrow and winding as this, but they were usually opened out by wire fencing. Here in Devon the high, spiky hedgerows towered so close to the road that she felt trapped in a maze.

The scene with Matthew Grieve played itself over and over again in her head. She hadn't meant to hurt him. In spite of her skills in the art of self-defence she had never used them in a real-life situation before.

Of course, she could have just sat around the house, patting Carl's hand and bemoaning cruel fate, but that wasn't her way. She was used to controlling situations. It had gone against the grain to wait passively for disaster, to allow two venal, self-seeking people to sacrifice Carl on the altar of Mammon. So she had *taken* control, attempted to get into that safe and away again with the least possible fuss. It was the guiding principle of judo: maximum efficiency, minimum effort, by which Jessica tried to live. She was usually successful in what she did. Knowing her own strengths and weaknesses meant that she rarely bit off more than she could chew.

Unfortunately this trip to England had introduced a variable, a hitherto unrealised flaw in her nature—recklessness. A desire to run before the wind, and hell-and-be-damned with respectability. But it hadn't been sheer recklessness that had got her into this impossible situation. It was love. Love for Carl, and Fiona, and poor, darling, innocent Maria.

Although he was only her stepbrother, Jessica felt closer to Carl than she had to any other human being. They had both been in their teens when their parents had married. Carl was four years older, and streets ahead of her intellectually, but Jessica had never felt patronised, or in the way. While he was at Medical School he had encouraged her efforts to start her own secretarial agency and it was to Carl, rather than her busy, impatient father, that she turned in times of strife. Now that their respective parents were dead, and Jessica's agency a runaway success, she felt a strong compulsion to show Carl her gratitude for all those years of caring and sharing.

She had missed Carl and Fiona terribly when they moved to England and when this chance had arisen, to travel to London as secretary to a man attending a series of international finance meetings, Jessica had leapt at it. With the job over she had caught the first train to Taunton, only to be met at the station by Fiona, with the disappointing news that her stepbrother had broken his leg in a fall a few days earlier.

'Don't be surprised if his temper's a bit surly,' Fiona told Jessica as she drove to their home in Barnstaple. 'He's been really looking forward to your coming but this leg has fouled things up. You know how he hates inactivity.'

Privately Jessica also wondered about Fiona, she seemed rather uptight about a simple broken leg. Were things not going too well for her? She had always been pale and delicate but at the moment she seemed more so than ever. If anyone deserved happiness, Fiona did.

Carl and Fiona had always wanted a family and when at last, three years ago, Fiona had fallen pregnant, they had been over the moon. But the pregnancy had been difficult and Fiona had been hysterical with grief and shock when she discovered that her beautiful new daughter had been born with Down's Syndrome. Carl's letters to Jessica during this time had been full of anguished bewilderment. Fiona seemed to have lost all sense of proportion, alternately blaming Carl and then herself for the tragedy, punishing them both by refusing to talk about it. Finally, after months of misery, she had a complete mental breakdown, rejecting both Carl and Maria as symbols of her failure. With care and therapy she had slowly recovered, becoming the warm and loving mother that she was destined to be.

Jessica was captivated by her first sight of Maria, a sweet toddler with a mop of fine blonde hair and the characteristic Mongol eyes—small and slanting and widely spaced. She was a cheerful, placid child and Fiona handled her beautifully, as if making up for the time when her own pain had overcome her maternal love.

In spite of Fiona's warning Jessica had had a shock on seeing her brother. He was older, greyer, tension lines scoring into his craggy face. As Jessica's three-week stay drew to an end she became more and more certain that something was very, very wrong. Carl and Fiona had done their best to entertain her but it was as if a cloud hung over the house and every now and then Jessica would glimpse desperation in their determined happiness. With the knowledge that time was running out, she risked a direct question when, mellowed by a good meal and two bottles of wine, they were least expecting it.

'Can't you tell me what's wrong? Or is it too personal? I might be able to help.'

There was a startled silence, and an immediate return to tension in the small room. Then, surprisingly, Fiona said: 'She's right, Carl. She might be able to help us.'

A line of red ran along Carl's cheekbones as he cast a long look at his wife. 'It was bad enough telling you,' he said, the words dragged out of him. 'But telling my sister too . . .'

'Then I'll tell her.' Fiona picked up Carl's clenched hand and held it tightly. 'What's a family for if not to share our troubles, and she might be able to see solutions we can't.'

Jessica listened, appalled, as her quiet, steady voice told the story.

During the months of turmoil leading up to Fiona's breakdown Carl had gone through a crisis of his own, despair that his marriage would not survive the tremendous pressures being placed upon it. Fiona didn't spare blame for herself, telling Jessica that she had rejected every overture that Carl had made to bridge the gap between them, and insisted that they sleep apart. But the echoes of the pain of betrayal were in her voice as she revealed that in his own search for meaning Carl had turned elsewhere, to a gay, sophisticated woman, totally unlike his wife. He had been briefly infatuated, the shock of Fiona's breakdown bringing home to him the stupidity of his actions.

'More than stupid,' Carl inserted, his voice thick with shame, his hand squeezing Fiona's tightly in return as he forced himself to take up the story, 'I was so bloody self-pitying I hadn't cared that I might be destroying the best thing in my life. Instead of having faith in Fiona, in our love, I acted like a selfish kid ... just when she needed me most. Thank God I came to my senses. It was part of Fiona's therapy that we go to marriage guidance and it was then I realised that if we were to have any chance of rebuilding I had to be totally honest. She was hurt and angry and bitter and thank God for my selfish soul she didn't forgive me too easily, but we worked it out.' Husband and wife smiled at each other, reaffirming their new trust.

But it didn't end there. Carl had written some letters which had fallen into the hands of his lover's husband—Matthew Grieve. He was now planning to use them in a divorce action, a course of action that would mean professional disaster for Carl. Lisa Grieve had once attended the practice as a patient and Carl would be struck off if their affair became known.

'If it comes out we'll lose everything ... the house, my share of the practice. If it was only me I'd tell him to go to hell, but there's Fiona—I've put her through enough already without subjecting her to that kind of scandal. And there's Maria ... I *need* my income if we're going to send her to a special school.'

He sounded like a man at the end of his tether and Fiona, too, looked frightened. Although she wore a new maturity, she was still undergoing some therapy and her strength was finite. Jessica listened to the rest with fatalistic calm.

Carl had gone to see Matthew Grieve, to plead the extenuating circumstances but he had been dismissed with callous indifference. It wasn't anger or jealousy that motivated the man, Carl claimed he had admitted he didn't give a damn who his wife slept with. For some time he had wanted to extricate himself from an increasingly expensive marriage and the letters would give him the perfect leverage to pare down the divorce settlement.

But Lisa Grieve wasn't willing. Painfully Carl gave a thumbnail sketch of the woman he had been infatuated with, expressing self-contempt as he did so. Lisa enjoyed the rank and privilege her marriage gave her, and if she was forced into forfeiting it she wanted to be generously compensated. She was going to contest, come hell or high water, and persuaded a desperate Carl that the only chance he had was to substitute innocent letters for the compromising ones her husband held.

'I thought, what the hell, I had nothing to lose,' said Carl half-defiantly 'and Fiona agreed with me.' He smiled tightly at Jessica's surprise. 'You don't think I could keep it a secret from her, do you? From now on every decision we make we make together.'

'But how *could* you agree?' asked a stunned Jessica of Fiona as she heard the plan. Lisa was going to give Carl a house key and the combination to her husband's safe, and turn off the alarm the morning the 'operation' was planned. She would then fly straight to Monte Carlo where she would remain until divorce proceedings began, trusting that her husband wouldn't find out about the letters until too late. With Matthew Grieve in Japan and his personal assistant away, Lisa was certain that nothing could go wrong.

'Because I'm not going to let her destroy Carl's life,' Fiona said grimly, her soft eyes steely. 'Whatever happens *she'll* be all right, the law sees to that, even if she doesn't get as much as she wants. But Carl won't. He'll have to pay over and over again for that mistake, we all will. And I don't think that's fair. It was as much her fault as his. To them its just a matter of money but it's our *life*.'

Jessica had her reservations but she could see Fiona's point . . . to her this must seem as though the affair was happening all over again. And Carl—Jessica looked at the anguished shame on his face—he too must be reliving an episode he would regret for the rest of his days. There and then she made up her mind.

'So that's why you're so uptight about your leg,' she said,' 'you can't very well go sprinting around the countryside in that cast. Someone else will have to do it for you.'

Of course they had argued. Jessica shouldn't get involved. They would cope. But she saw the quick leap of relief in Carl's eyes before he smothered it with protests and the edge of hope that clipped Fiona's speech. With Carl immobile Jessica had taken charge and told them that she was going ahead, regardless of their approval, and that they couldn't stop her.

'As Fiona said—what's a family for?' said Jessica, all her loyalties rising to bolster her determination. She didn't condone Carl's infidelity, but she didn't condemn it, either, knowing he had been under a fearful strain at the time. That he was truly remorseful was obvious ... there would never be a second fall from grace. 'This is all due to happen, when?—in two days?' Carl nodded defeatedly. 'Well, there's no time to change all the plans ... I'll just have to modify them a bit.'

Carl tried to dissuade her right up until the last moment but Fiona, once she had decided she was on Jessica's side, helped without comment or question, her small face stubbornly set. Jessica had the feeling that if she hadn't been there Fiona would have tried it herself, whatever the cost to her nerves. She needed the security of her family so very much that she was every bit as desperate as Carl.

There were no Pandas or flashing lights. Jessica hardly met a car on the road until she entered Barnstaple, skirting the town centre to draw up outside the small semi-detached where her brother lived.

'Well? How did it go?' Carl and Fiona were waiting, pale and tense, as soon as she walked in the door. Jessica knew that she wasn't going to tell them about Matthew Grieve, not until she knew for certain the complications involved. Let them have their peace of mind, even if it be brief.

'Like a dream,' she said, warming herself by the fire. More like a nightmare. 'I'm thinking of taking up safe-cracking as a living.'

'Don't even joke about it,' Carl collapsed back in his chair in relief while Fiona got them all stiff whiskys. 'And the letters?'

'Burnt.' Jessica took her drink and smiled crookedly as she toasted: 'To crime.'

'To the quiet life,' Fiona responded wryly and they all sipped liberally.

Jessica felt the liquor burn down her throat and sear away some of her fear, though her hands still trembled very slightly.

'I suppose I should have asked this before,' she said slowly, 'but couldn't Lisa Grieve have come up with a counter-threat to shut her husband up? If they've been living separate lives, surely there were other women ...' The man in the doorway might have been rumpled and unshaven but there had been a certain animal attraction about him. The way he had looked at her ... the way he had kissed her. She gulped some more whisky, blaming it for the warmth that spread in her stomach when she remembered the touch of his mouth, the rough texture of his hand when he had stroked her. She had been too close to panic then to react with anything more than shock, but now her knees went weak at the image of the two of them, strangers, locked in a sensuous embrace in the silent room. She cursed herself for opening another line of conversation, when what she really wanted was for Carl and Fiona to go up to bed so that she could use the telephone.

'According to Lisa he hasn't had time,' Carl looked awkwardly at Fiona. 'He's a workaholic, always at the office or away on business. Never takes her. Didn't want a family. Lisa was really bitter about that.'

Jessica exchanged a startled look with Fiona, seeing in her sister-in-law's eyes a faint cynicism that said it all. Lisa Grieve didn't sound like the kind of woman who pines for the ties of hearth and home, but Carl obviously believed it. Perhaps it was necessary to his pride to believe some good about a woman who had used him for her own ends. Of course, Carl had also used her . . . and Jessica sensed that that was as great a source of shame to him as the fact of his infidelity. Infatuation wasn't love, and often it was a mask for even less finer feelings.

'Why didn't she just get pregnant?' asked Jessica.

Carl frowned. 'She thought of that . . . said she probably would have ended up on the street, with him denying paternity. He doesn't take kindly to being crossed.'

Now *that* Jessica could believe.

'I still think she should have tried to find out if he has been straying as well.' She winced as she realised what she had said, but Fiona just gave her a grave smile. 'How long have they been married?'

'Nine years. And she did. She couldn't penetrate the business Mafia.' Carl swallowed the rest of his drink. 'Maybe he has got a discreet mistress somewhere, but who's going to inform on a man who can turn around and ruin you? He's in property development and all sorts of things. Chews up his enemies and spits them out, says Lisa.'

Jessica's spine went icy cold. She was his enemy

now, or she would be when he found out what she had done.

It occurred to them all at the same time.

'We shouldn't have let you do it,' said Carl.

'Well, it's over now. Finished,' said Jessica firmly, hoping against hope that it was, feeling the magnetic attraction of the telephone across the room. 'Let's just forget it ever happened. You two look as exhausted as I feel, why don't you go on up and I'll damp the fire?'

To her relief they did, Fiona after a brief hug that spoke volumes, and Carl lingering for a gruff goodnight. It made it all worth while to see the old gleam in his eyes.

'Never again, Jessica. Never again,' he vowed with a raw sincerity that caught at her heart.

She waited until she heard the shuffle-clunk, shuffle-clunk of his unwieldly gait along the hallway over her head before she moved towards the kitchen phone. She slid out the telephone directory and leafed through it, momentarily afraid that he would have an unlisted number.

No, there it was, M. J. Grieve. She broke a nail dialing and waited, palms sweating furiously as she listened to the tone ring . . . and ring . . . and ring. If he was dead, would the police think it was an accident? Please, *please* let him be all right!

Matthew Grieve opened his eyes and stared at the ornate plaster ceiling. He frowned and shifted his head, wincing at the thumping pain. His mouth was arid and foul. One hell of a hangover. Why was the bed so hard? Not bed . . . floor. Had he fallen? This wasn't his bedroom. Why was he so cold? He raised his head an inch and groaned out loud. God, his head hurt. Vodka didn't usually give him a hangover. He'd had none on the flight from Japan and no more than usual on the long drive home, as he worked in the back seat of the Rolls. So why was he feeling so bad? It was a sharp, stabbing pain rather than the usual dull throb a hangover caused. He rolled painfully on to his side, nearly knocking over the glass that stood on the rug a few inches away. He stared at it, baffled. Had he been so drunk that he passed out on the floor? The drink wavered and he blinked rapidly, focused on the blob of red beside it. A rose? He grabbed it, crushing it in his fingers. Not real, yet perfumed. He raised it to his face and inhaled the fragrance . . . it brought with it a hazy memory.

He shook his head and groaned again. There had been a woman. A beautiful woman, perfumed like the rose. One of John's women, though not quite in his usual style, and she'd hit him for kissing her. No . . . that wasn't right. *She* had kissed *him*. And she hadn't hit him, she'd thrown him. A judo throw that had caught him completely off balance. He must have hit his head as he fell.

He sat up and stared around the room. Had he been hallucinating? Lack of sleep could do that to a man, and he hadn't had anything but a short nap for the past seventy-two hours.

No. His hand clenched around the crushed rose. She'd been here all right, the evidence was in his hand . . . and, painfully, on the back of his head. Who was she? What had she been after, that beautiful, lethal lady? Not so much of the lady, he amended cynically, remembering the practised way she had vamped him, flaunting those magnificent breasts . . . even the memory was capable of distracting him. He remembered how surprisingly soft her mouth had been, in spite of her boldness, the scent of her rising in his nostrils, the warm weight of her breast in his palm, the sensuous slide of her thigh against his.

Clever. She had been very clever. Obviously she had lied about being a friend of John's. Her dress, her

manner, had fooled him completely. Matthew rose to
his feet, staggering slightly as he crossed over to the
safe. The effects of the blow were beginning to wear
off and his mind was reeling out the possibilities.

A moment later he was leaning against the desk,
surveying the room with dark-eyed perplexity. The
safe was undisturbed. The displays of porcelain and
silver were intact. There was nothing missing from the
desk. The Turner? He looked at the painting. She had
mentioned it. Had she come here to steal it, and fled
when he caught her in the act? He swallowed the sour
taste in his mouth as his tired brain grappled with the
problem.

There were any number of reasons she might have
been here. Some of his opponents wouldn't baulk at a
little industrial espionage but, fortunately, there were
no sensitive papers at his house; they were in a well-
guarded office in London.

Still puzzling, he walked over to the brandy glass on
the rug and picked it up, taking a sip from the
contents. Thoughtful bitch ... to knock him out and
then leave a reviver. And the rose? Why had she left
that? To taunt him? Mock him with his helplessness?
God, physically subdued by a woman!—what a field
day his enemies would have with that one! Matthew
swore fluently. For a man used to being the dominant
partner in any relationship, it was an unpleasant lesson
in humility. The fact that he had been tired, off-guard,
was no excuse.

He had been asleep when something had woken him
in the austere bedroom on the second floor. He
guessed that his overall exhaustion had had a lot to do
with the ease with which he had been vanquished. He
wondered about calling the police, but decided to
leave that decision until he had discovered whether
anything was missing, and found out whether his
nocturnal visitor *had* gained access through John. He

certainly didn't relish informing the local police of the incident. The press would have a field day. However ... he did have one or two contacts higher up who might be able to arrange a discreet investigation. He spun round groggily at the telephone on the desk rang. He was expecting no calls. He picked up the phone, cursing as he fumbled the receiver and almost cut the connection.

'Grieve.'

There was silence at the other end and he waited patiently, used to such delays on international calls.

'Are you all right?' The husky voice sounded so near he started. It wasn't an international call after all. He didn't recognise the voice, or understand the question.

'You must have the wrong number.'

'Matthew Grieve?' Low, almost a whisper, but the inflection tugged at his memory.

'Yes. Who is this?'

'Are you all right?'

'Yes, of course I am. Who is this?' he demanded, impatient with the evasion.

'Are you sure? Have you called a doctor?'

'What?'

'You might have concussion.'

His mind made the quantum leap to understanding. He remembered the husky voice now, and the wide, red mouth from whence it had issued. He couldn't believe her audacity.

'Where are you calling from? Who are you?' he demanded harshly. It wasn't enough that this woman had violated his house and disposed of him as if he was a weakling child. She now had the gall to ring and rub his nose in it. His temper, slow to rise but wicked in its intensity, overrode his commonsense. 'What the hell do you want?'

'I was worried about you. I thought you might still

be unconscious.' Matthew ground his teeth at the spurious note of concern. She hadn't been so concerned when she flipped him out of her way.

'The hell you did,' he grated enraged by his impotence. He had a sudden, satisfying, searing, vision of his hands locked around that bejewelled neck, squeezing the truth out of her. 'Who are you? What do you want?'

'Have you called a doctor, I think you should. I wouldn't like to have your death on my conscience.'

'Your conscience!' With an effort Matthew controlled his urge to slam the receiver down. He was finding out nothing and he was damned if he was going to let this woman get the better of him yet again. He attempted a more reasonable tone. 'I'll call a doctor, I'd already decided to. What were you doing here? What is it you were after? The Turner? I haven't called the police ... yet. I might not, if you co-operate.'

There was a pause at the other end of the line, a quick breath which could have been a gasp or a laugh. Matthew stared savagely at the crumpled rose on the desk. If he could just manipulate her into revealing a clue it would provide a starting point for the investigation. He was very practised at controlling people and had a photographic memory. He never forgot a face, or a name ... or a voice. He never forgot an injury, either.

A low, teasing laugh caressed his ear and the reply came, velvety with provocation.

'Why, haven't you guessed yet?' Another laugh, filled with a soft exultation that sent his blood pressure rocketting with fury. 'I'm *Love*, Matthew Grieve. And I came to steal your heart!'

There was a click and Matthew was left with silence. For an instant he lost grip on reality, her words echoing weirdly in his brain. Had she indeed

been some supernatural manifestation, come to haunt
him at the sterile end of a loveless mockery of a
marriage?

He jerked upright with a vicious oath. She was
doing it again ... clouding his reason. *Love!* Greed,
more like; another beautiful, grasping woman who
wanted to take without giving, who was never satisfied
with what she had. Bitch! She had been laughing at
him, enjoying his impotence. He lifted the receiver
again and dialled. No one, *no one*, got away with
taunting Matt Grieve! He would find her, however
long it took, and wipe that smile off her face. She had
two traits he couldn't stomach in a woman—
aggressiveness and dishonesty—and he would take
the greatest pleasure in crushing both underfoot. He
was not normally sadistic, but the idea of having her
under his physical domination was extraordinarily
satisfying. To have her on her knees before him,
beautiful face streaked with tears of humiliation as
she submissively begged for forgiveness ... God, he
would enjoy that! He smiled grimly. Perhaps she had
stolen something from him after all ... not his
heart, that was too well-guarded, but a measure of
his masculinity. Well, he would have it back ...
with interest!

Jessica hung up, aghast at her foolishness. Why had
she added that last, outrageous remark? Why had she
taunted him? What would she want with his heart,
anyway ... a lump of valueless rock?

She bit her lip as she remembered his words: '*I might
not, if you co-operate*'. He had not fooled her for a
minute. Under that silky reason had been a deadly fury,
but she had felt safe at the other end of the anonymous
line. Even if he did call the police, what would they find?
It probably wouldn't occur to them, or to Matthew
Grieve, to check the *inside* of those envelopes.

She had satisfied her main concern, that he wasn't dead. Now she must take the same, sound advice she had given to Carl. Forget it—it never happened.

CHAPTER FOUR

THE party had begun quietly but as the night wore on it began to degenerate into a noisy free-for-all. The crush was enormous, everyone shrieking at each other over the pounding beat of a live band. The air was thick with cigarette smoke and a heavier, more distinctly scented haze that Jessica appreciated even less. She didn't need chemicals to enhance her enjoyment of life. Judo kept her fit, kept her mentally as well as physically in condition. Its credos encouraged self-control and self-knowledge—you didn't find those in the bottom of a glass or at the end of a joint.

Jessica coughed as she inhaled another waft of somebody else's poison. Michael, her escort, was deep in discussion with a fellow guest and she listened half-heartedly, thinking that although he had proved to be a very pleasant companion over the past year or so, he was also rather boringly bland. He was too nice for his own good. But then, Jessica found most men boring. After her one disastrous foray into love when still a schoolgirl she had turned her back on romantic nonsense. She had absorbed herself in her career and firmly shelved all girlish notions of home and family. That would come later, when the agency's demands on her time lessened, when she could look around for the kind of man she thought she could spend the rest of her life with.

Exactly what kind of man that was she wasn't sure. But she knew what he would *not* be. He wouldn't be like Michael, who was a bit of a jellyfish, always willing to compromise his opinions for her sake. But neither would he be domineering, the way her father had been. Jessica couldn't remember her own mother, who had died when she was two, but the way her forceful father had taken her stepmother for granted had appalled her. And Linda had accepted his dominance as a matter of course.

No, the kind of man Jessica envisaged as attracting her was strong yet capable of tenderness, self-confident but not overconfident, even-tempered and respectful of her rights as a woman. She had not yet met a man who came even close to that image, but Jessica wasn't worried. At the moment her life was quite fulfilling as it was.

She slipped her feet out of her shoes with a sigh. Monday was always a bad day, the phones running hot as clients scrambled to sign up their favourite temps for the gaps left by cases of extended 'Mondayitis'. Business was expanding so rapidly that she and Jill were considering investing some of their hard-earned profits in a computer to handle the workload. Meanwhile, with just three of them in the office, every minute of every day was crammed with activity.

Jessica thrived on the challenge. Her upbringing and the struggle to start a business in what was essentially a man's world had given her a smooth veneer of confidence. She had gained respect from others and that in turn had boosted her self-respect. If, deep down, she had any doubts, they were well concealed from general view. It was dangerous to admit one's weaknesses, it gave them light to grow. So Jessica tried not to think about the possibility that she might one day come up against a situation, a person, that she couldn't handle. And the probability that that person would be a man. For men possessed a secret weapon; secret, at least, to Jessica. Sex. It had been ineffective against her in the past but it wouldn't remain so forever. Some day she was going to feel a very powerful attraction towards a man. She could only hope that her strength of mind would ensure that he was suitably deserving of her love.

Jessica shook her head slightly as a vision rose—a dark, angry man with warm insistent hands. Now why should she think of Matthew Grieve?

She squared her shoulders, arching her tired back and quickly looked away from a young man on her left whose eyes gleamed at the stretch of green fabric across her breasts. Men were so obvious. Her eyes collided with a dark pair across the crowded room and for a moment she felt hot and dizzy. Little fireflies of puzzlement danced hectically across her vision.

It couldn't be.

She stared. Matthew Grieve. Leaning casually against the wall there, as if her wayward thoughts had conjured flesh from unwelcome fantasy. Matthew Grieve, or his twin brother.

He was smiling at her vaguely, as one does at a face one feels one should recognise. Jessica longed to look away, but she couldn't tear her horrified gaze from his. She saw the exact moment of realisation ... the confirmation of his identity. All at once he was alert, smile swallowed up in sheer, incredulous fury. Fifteen metres away Jessica felt the blast of heat like a physical slap on the face. She watched, rooted to the floor, as he drew himself up and launched into the mass of people between them, pushing and shoving, never taking his obsidian eyes off her.

Jessica took to her heels, or at least she tried to. First she had to find them. She bent and scrabbled on the floor. Cramming her feet into her shoes she tried to wriggle her way through the tightly packed crowd, ignoring Michael's questioning remark. She had to make it to the stairs. The house was big and old, with lots of little rooms and odd corners, plenty of places to hide out for a while.

Grimly she battled on, ignoring the complaints as she jostled her way into the hall, feeling a terrible desire to scream and claw at the barrier of bodies. She could sense him behind her, *feel* the waves of pure menace beating at her back. She risked a glance behind her. Oh, God he was being even rougher than she was, zeroing in on her flushed and desperate escape like a heat-seeking missile.

She almost made it, but she stumbled on the fifth stair.

'Oh no you don't!' An angry hand caught the swirling pleats of her skirt as she regained her balance, and wrenched hard. Jessica spun around, falling against the bannister.

'I want to talk to you!'

Jessica went white at the expression on his face, a look of savage expectancy that scared her more than outright fury would have done. He didn't look as if words would satisfy him. What was he going to do? Expose her in front of all these people? She trembled at the thought of such humiliation.

For a moment they remained frozen in an aggressive tableau, linked to reality by the hard grasp of his hand, minds and emotions slipping into the past, to their last confrontation. Jessica's lips parted but no words came out, dried up by the bitter triumph that glittered in his dark eyes, the formality of his dark suit and white shirt contrasting with the emotion stripped bare on the hard, patrician face.

She backed up a stair on trembling legs, trying to pull the fullness of her skirt away from his grip. He remained where he was, the fabric straining between them, a diabolical smile splintering across the cold mouth.

'Do that and I'll tear it off you!' It sounded like a dare, as if he wanted her to try and get away so that he could carry out his threat.

'Let me go,' she whispered rigidly, clenching her hands at her side, leaning back but not daring to move, to provoke him.

'Never.' He savoured the word, winding his fist deeper into the silk pleats, inexorably tightening his grip so that Jessica felt the stitches begin to strain and pop. Oh, God! Tonight there was no weakness or dissipation about him. He wasn't weary, off-guard. If he had been drinking it had been only enough to put an invidious edge on his temper. 'We have an old score to settle . . . *Love.*'

The snarling endearment went through Jessica like ice. She struggled to regain her senses, benumbed by the ghastly nightmare. A woman came down the stairs past them, giving the frozen pair a curious look and Jessica suddenly thought . . . if I could make everyone look—and not just look!

She raised two fingers to her mouth and gave a piercing whistle that penetrated the jam-packed hall below.

'Hey everybody!' she shouted in a high-pitched voice as faces began to turn upwards. 'Guess what! It's Matt's birthday today, and nobody's realised. How about a smothering of kisses and champagne to cheer the poor darling up!'

She couldn't have chosen a more perfect psychological moment if she had tried. The party spirit was beginning to sag and this was just the kind of boisterous lift that was needed.

Matthew Grieve swore at her under his breath and leapt up the stairs, dragging Jessica up with him. But the crowd below was too many for him, rising in a laughing tide, surrounding them, sweeping them back downstairs, shouting congratulations.

Crushed together in the middle of the melee Jessica tried to twist away from the inflexible hand. Someone shook up a champagne bottle and foam began to fly to the accompaniment of shrieks of merriment. Matthew Grieve was cursing out loud now, yelling at the revellers, but most of them seemed too drunk to notice his unwillingness to join in the fun.

Jessica was almost sobbing in frustration. The man was so damned single-minded he still hadn't let go of her dress, he was hanging on like grim death. As a last resort she lowered her head and bit him, hard, on the wrist. His hand loosened and she wrenched free and dropped to the floor, crawling through the swaying forest of legs which barred her way. She emerged bruised and shattered, on the other side of the noisy mass of people.

She didn't know where Michael had got to and didn't care. She fell out into the dark street, lifting her ankle-length skirt to dash across the road and round the first corner she came to. She didn't relish walking strange streets at this time of night but it was infinitely preferable to going back to face Matthew Grieve's justifiable wrath. The look on his face! She had stopped at the doorway and looked back, just in time to see him hoisted on a dozen shoulders, a busty blonde trailing from his waist. He had seen her too, on the verge of escaping him a second time, and his eyes had promised black murder. She scooted around another dark corner, as if the devil himself were on her trail. She must find a telephone booth.

As it happened, she didn't need to find one. A taxi cruised by and she waved at it gratefully, scrambling in when it pulled over to the kerb and sinking low in the seat. She gave the grizzled, overweight driver her address.

'And could you make it as fast as you can?'

'Trouble?' She could see him surreptitiously checking her over in his mirror.

'I hope not,' she muttered, clutching the seat as the tyres squealed a U-turn.

To forestall further comments she opened the tiny purse that folded over her belt and drew out her compact. She was horrified to see traces of blood at the corner of her mouth . . . no wonder the driver had given her that odd look. She wiped the dark spot off with a tissue. *His* blood; she could actually taste it on her tongue. She must have marked him . . . punctured his skin. Like a vampire. And now they were forever bound by blood-thrall.

Jessica snapped her compact and put it away. Idiot! Sounding like a B-grade horror movie. If he had let her go she wouldn't have had to bite him. Why was it she was always *having* to do terrible things to Matthew Grieve? A total stranger. Well, almost total.

She couldn't credit the coincidence. It had to be that because it was obvious from his shock that he hadn't been expecting to see her. But what was he doing in New Zealand? Surely Carl would have warned her if he was aware of any further repercussions from that night in Devon?

Neither of them had mentioned the subject in their letters over the past year, not since Carl had sent her a cutting from one of the English Sunday papers. Jessica had winced at the strident style of the report. The Grieves' divorce had been granted on the grounds of irreconcilable differences—no juicy scandal there—but the paper had made up for it in picking over the details of the settlement. Lisa had demanded, and got, a lump sum—plus the house in Devon, the Rolls Royce, jewellery, and a villa in Monte Carlo. Jessica had gasped at the paper's crude estimate of Lisa's financial worth as an ex-wife.

Her knowledge had doubled her fright this evening. By now Matthew Grieve must have made the connection, or at least have a shrewd suspicion of why she had been in his house that night. He hadn't informed the police at the time, Carl had written her that much, but perhaps, since the divorce, he had instituted a private investigation?

As soon as she got home she would ring Carl and find out why Matthew Grieve was out of England. No. She was too upset tonight; she might inadvertently blurt everything out! She would wait until the morning, call him from the office, pretend mild, if anxious, interest.

The trouble was that if Matthew Grieve was on the warpath there wasn't a lot she could do about it. This was home. She couldn't run away. She had responsibilities.

There was an advantage in that it had been a big party, with no formal guest list. And there had been plenty of women wearing green. Jessica didn't flatter herself that she had stood out in the crowd of beautifully dressed females ... except to a man who had good reason to notice her.

'Here you are then, safe and sound.' The taxi driver twisted round in his seat to tell her the fare.

Jessica handed him the money and began to get out. Suddenly she had a thought. 'Look, if anyone asks ... I mean I'd rather not ... if anyone wants to know where you took me ...' she tailed off, wondering if she was sounding criminal.

'Making a nuisance of himself is he?'

'Is he ever!' said Jessica, thankful for the excuse. It was true, but not in the way the driver meant.

'Well, mum's the word. He won't find out anything from me.'

'Thanks,' Jessica gave him a dazzlingly grateful smile.

'Can't say I blame him, though.' The man chuckled as she walked up the path to the small block of flats.

She let herself into the ground-floor unit quietly, not wanting to face a friendly interrogation from Jill. Her flatmate and business partner was also her closest friend, but even Jill didn't know about Jessica's little venture into crime.

She did go and have a shower, though, to wash away the scent of fear. She wished it was as easy to wash away the other disturbing feelings. Why should she feel any guilt? There was no shame in being loyal to your family.

It's because I always sympathise with the underdog, she told herself as the water slicked down over her body. Once Carl was out from under, it was Matthew Grieve who had been the underdog. He was, after all, the innocent party in the sordid triangle ... or relatively innocent. By trickery and deceit he had been deprived of his beautiful home, his masculine pride and a great deal of money. There was all that speculative publicity, too, over the divorce. Jessica tried to banish the tentative tendrils of sympathy by reminding herself how callously Matthew Grieve had behaved towards Carl.

'Have a good time? You look terrible.' Jill Waverly pushed a cup of coffee across the breakfast table.

'Good party, terrible night,' Jessica groaned, feeling as if her head was stuffed with straw. She sipped her coffee. She had had that dream again, the one where she was lost in a big, dark house, searching for something vital. This time she had felt another presence as she roamed from room to room. Something dark, predatory, waiting in the shadows, feeding on her fear.

'You won't want any eggs then?' Jill was a superb cook and did most of their meals while Jessica, a more orderly soul, did the cleaning and laundry.

'No, thank you,' Jessica shuddered. She wouldn't be able to stomach anything heavier than coffee until she had put that call through to Carl.

'Well, I'll spare your hangover and have toast

myself,' said Jill and Jessica smiled wanly at the plump redhead as she moved around the small kitchen. They were well-attuned to each other's moods and rarely were there cross words between them.

It had been a lucky day for Jessica when, four years ago, Jill had turned up at the Agency seeking a job. The thirty-eight-year-old divorcée had been re-entering the work force after eighteen years of marriage. Her husband had traded in his *hausfrau* for a younger career woman and Jill was determined to prove that she wasn't over the hill yet. She had picked herself up, dusted off her secretarial skills, learned word-processing and started studying accountancy part-time.

Jessica had put her on the books and watched with growing admiration as Jill polished her image. A lot of employers preferred a mature woman in their offices, someone who took adversity calmly in her stride, and Jill fitted the bill perfectly. She also discovered that she was enjoying her new independence for its own sake, and looked for even more challenges.

It was at this point that the two women had made their bargain. They had become good friends and one day Jessica confided that, though the Wright Agency was gaining a reputation in Auckland's business community for providing high quality, reliable office staff, youthful energy and ambition could take her only so far. It had taken Jessica years to build up her clientele but if she was to consolidate and expand she needed capital, and someone to share the growing responsibilities of ownership.

The tacit offer was taken up with alacrity. Jill had bought a partnership, qualified for her accountancy diploma, and taken over the financial management of the Wright-Waverly Agency. Jessica had never regretted allowing her friend to share her dream. Her own academic record at school was mediocre, she had been far more interested in sport than schoolwork, and she had known for some time that certain aspects of the business needed the attention of someone with Jill's head for figures. Jessica herself concentrated on the human side, interviewing job applicants, matching the right person to the right job, and touting for business. Since they had combined their talents the Agency's profits had soared and they had expanded their operation to provide a permanent as well as temporary employment service.

'If you feel that bad, why don't you come in later?' offered Jill as Jessica continued to stare morosely into her coffee. 'I can hold the fort this morning.'

'Thanks, but I'd rather work.' In the past she had always been able to put aside personal considerations once she got to the office.

They took their separate cars to work and by the time Jessica entered their small, bright, central-city office she was feeling a trifle calmer. May as well face fate with a smile.

'Morning, Kay,' she greeted their competent, dark-haired receptionist. 'Any calls for me?'

'Only one, from that girl we sent to the construction company. Another complaint.'

'Damn, that's the second time in two months. Does she want to make it official?'

'No. She just wants another job.'

'Neither did the other girl. I suppose *I'll* have to take it on.'

'If he's tall, dark and handsome, why not send me to investigate?' joked Kay, although they all took complaints about sexual harassment seriously. Usually Jessica gave the employer the benefit of the doubt by taking on the next job request from him herself. If the complaint was justified she bumped the offender from

her books and did her best to encourage the signing of
an official complaint, particularly where the man was
with a large company, and in a position to make life
miserable for any number of women employees.

Jessica read the report on her desk and rang the
young secretary concerned before she returned to her
own problems. She direct-dialled Carl's number and
waited anxiously as the tone rang.

'Dr McKenzie's residence.'

'Carl?'

'Jessica! You must be psychic, I was just going to
ring you.' His voice was packed with suppressed
excitement and Jessica's stomach plunged.

'What's happened? What's wrong?'

'Nothing's *wrong* ... everything's right. Fiona's
pregnant again! Jessica ... Jessica? Are you there?
Hello?'

Jessica found her tongue. 'Yes, yes ... sorry, you
took my breath away for a moment. Congratulations!
How far along?'

'Four months. Sorry I didn't let you know before
but Fiona wanted to be sure first that everything was
OK.'

'And is it?'

'Yep. She's had every test it's possible to have and
the baby is fine.' His voice was thick with relief.
Jessica could imagine the torments they had both gone
through imagining that this child, too, might be
handicapped. They would still worry, of course, until
the baby arrived safely, but at least their worst fears
had been laid to rest.

'I'm so pleased for you, Carl. It's fantastic. How's
Fiona?'

'Retching her heart out every morning, poor love,
but she's not sick all day like she was last time. I'm
making sure she takes it easy ... no emotional upsets,
no heavy housework. She seems to be a lot stronger

this time, thank goodness, but I just wish the next five months were over and done with!'

'Don't you dare! It'll take me that long to knit a pair of booties.' Jessica hated knitting.

Carl's laugh boomed across the world. 'Don't bother—the last pair you did were so lumpy that they gave poor Maria corns.'

'Pig!' Jessica's laughter died as she remembered the reason for her call. 'Carl . . . I ran across Matthew Grieve yesterday.'

There was a sudden silence at the end of the line.

'That's why I called, actually. I wondered if you knew what he was doing in New Zealand. You don't think he might have . . .?'

'No, no, of course he hasn't, how could he?' Carl cut in reassuringly. 'He never found out about the switch until weeks after you left, and I don't think he ever connected me with it . . . if he had I'm sure I wouldn't be talking to you so happily now. Even if the worst came to the worst, why should you be involved? We've got different surnames, you don't even have to admit you know me. When you say "ran across" . . .?'

'I saw him at a party, that's all,' Jessica hurried in with the lie. It was too late to confess all now. 'So you don't think he's still harbouring a grudge?'

'Well, I don't think he was too pleased the way things worked out,' said Carl drily. 'He gave Lisa a pretty rough time in court over the settlement. The press were buzzing like flies around them and Lisa didn't help matters by blabbing a sob story to a couple of reporters. He apparently hired private detectives to watch her in Monte Carlo; that must have been after he found out about the letters.'

'Oh, God!' Jessica felt sick at the thought of all the poking and prying. 'He must have been desperate.'

'To no avail, anyway. She must have lived the life of

a nun until the hearing. That would have been a severe strain, I'll bet.'

No trace of infatuation there, thought Jessica wryly. 'I'm surprised he didn't toss your name to the wolves out of sheer spite when he realised that he wasn't going to be able to produce evidence of adultery in court.'

'He still could, I suppose . . . it only takes a whisper to the B.M.A. and even if I was cleared some mud would stick. Maybe Lisa exaggerated that side of his character a bit, to egg me on. I guess he's the kind of guy who likes to cut his losses . . . on the rare occasions that he *does* lose. Anyway, he wasn't a broken man, you know. He *wanted* to get rid of Lisa and he's still rolling in it. What with the rate of inflation he probably benefits from giving her a lump sum. If they'd stayed married she would have cost him even more.'

'So we really did him a favour,' Jessica said sarcastically, although there was a grain of truth in what Carl said.

'Oh, it was wrong, Jess, I'm not excusing myself. I was bloody stupid and I almost paid for it in blood. But . . . what's done is done and I owe it to Fiona and Maria and the new baby to make the best of it.'

'Well, I'll let you go back to your beauty sleep——'

'Give me a break, I've just come back from a call! Great to hear your voice, Jess, and you can expect a letter from Fiona any day now, and a scribble or two from Maria.'

''Bye Carl.'

Jessica put the phone down, comforted but not totally reassured by Carl's words. He wasn't in full possession of the facts—he didn't realise that the recognition had been mutual. Matthew Grieve might be a man to cut his losses, but what if he saw a chance to redeem them!

Jessica had barely time to recover from one unsettling telephone call than she had another. This time it was Michael, quite rightly upset that she had abandoned him without a word last night. Embarrassed that she had forgotten all about him she soothed him as best she could and promised to have dinner with him later in the week.

Men! It seemed all her current problems revolved around men. How pleasantly uncomplicated women were in comparison! And what a pompous, absurd generalisation *that* was, Jessica admonished herself as she tried to concentrate on the list of prospective secretaries who had applied to be registered with the Agency. Jessica was strongly feminist, but not anti-men, as some of the fanatics were. Nor did she blindly believe that men and women were completely equal. But she did believe that feminine endeavour and achievement were consistently underrated and under-encouraged for all sorts of reasons—from biological to economic.

Her own background was a prime example. Her father had allowed her to be brought up by a succession of housekeepers before Linda came along, and had held very low expectations of his daughter. Without Carl's support during the confusing, adolescent years, Jessica might well have been the failure her father expected her to be. That's why on the spur of the moment, she had been prepared to risk everything for him. And still was.

CHAPTER FIVE

IF Matthew Grieve had been trying to find her he hadn't had any success, Jessica decided, eight nerve-racking days later. Discreet enquiry had elicited the information that his interests in New Zealand revolved around hotel syndicates and electronics. None of the companies with which he had investments were clients of Wright-Waverly so there was no danger of his making a connection in that area either. Jessica settled down to sleeping nights again.

'I think you'd better handle him, Jessica. He just won't listen to me. Stubborn as a mule. And he sent the last girl back in tears.'

'What does he expect from us, Superwoman?' Jessica demanded of an exasperated Kay. 'How many is that now?'

Kay consulted the file in her hand. 'Four, including Katherine May.' Katherine was one of their best temps, with top shorthand and typing speeds. A most equable, efficient secretary. Jessica couldn't imagine a situation arising with which Katherine couldn't cope.

'What's the matter with the man? His credentials checked out perfectly. Nobody said he was a monster!'

'Trouble?' Jill strolled into Jessica's office with a sheaf of invoices.

'It's this construction engineer from New Guinea. He's putting too much pressure on . . . none too polite about it either. The way he's treating our staff I wouldn't be too surprised if he runs through our entire listing. He's impossible to please.'

'Tell him to rent a dictaphone and word processor,' said Jill brightly, being in the midst of learning about micro-technology herself, so that she could choose the computer best suited to the Agency's needs.

'Not good enough,' said Jessica drily. 'He apparently wants a good old-fashioned secretary so that he can do some good, old-fashioned ego-tripping.'

'Really, Jessica, if he's going to keep carrying on like this I don't feel we can in all fairness recommend him to the girls. He was most offensive on the telephone just now.'

Jessica frowned. 'He sent in such a good reference from Sprion Construction with his letter that I didn't bother to run any further checks. I can't understand it, Spiron have never recommended a dud to us before.'

'Well, what do you want me to do? Do you want me to give him the bird?' asked Kay, with a certain amount of relish.

'Of course she doesn't, do you, Jess?' grinned Jill knowingly. Jessica had never been known to cop out on a contract, not for the sake of a mere man's bad temper.

'No, damn it, let's find out what he *really* wants! Four temps in as many days—that's a record! And that's definitely as far as it goes. I presume he wants someone for tomorrow?'

'Seared my eardrums with it,' Kay confirmed, her young face admiring of Jessica's courage. 'And *this* time, send him *someone* who knows what the word work *means*.'

'I'll sort out Mr——' Jessica squinted at the file card, '—Mr Martin Gibson. He's not going to bully round *my* people. You get on the telephone and tell him that I'll be coming, *personally*.'

'You'd better wear some armour plating, then,' said Kay, relieved to be off the hook. 'He has a mouth like a machine gun.'

'Well, I'm about to jam his magazine,' said Jessica grimly, to her partner's delight. Good businesswoman that she was, Jill had too soft a heart to tackle the kind of problems that Jessica excelled at.

Accordingly the next morning Jessica was armoured in a beautifully tailored blue suit and blue checked blouse with contrasting turn-back French cuffs and collar. Her hair she had gathered away from her face in a loose, but firmly anchored knot. As she walked through the city streets she savoured the light spring breeze, her long, straight-backed stride drawing some admiring glances. Jessica was proud of her height. She had never, even in her early teens, felt the need to hide it by slouching. Pride in oneself was half the battle in life.

Even the elevator in the Cheshire Building was plush, she thought, as she pressed the button for the fifth floor. It was carpeted—floor, walls and ceiling—in warm apricot, with a mirror inset on the side wall. Jessica checked her appearance—no-nonsense yet attractive, just the look she had been aiming for. The light of battle gave an added sparkle to her hazel eyes. Perversely she was looking forward to a confrontation, rather hoping that Mr Martin Gibson wouldn't be soothed by her professionalism. She had been feeling tired and jumpy all week, maybe a good fight would clear out her system!

She got no answer from her knock on the door of suite 523 so she strode in of her own accord. The single desk in the large, modern reception room was nearly empty, only a typewriter on it, and a telephone. Jessica raised her eyebrows. Gibson must certainly believe in spartan working conditions.

There were three other doors leading off the room, all ajar. Jessica looked into the first. This room wasn't even furnished with a desk—wall-to-wall carpet in jarring green and a forlorn telephone sitting dustily on the floor. Door number two yielded the same result. Jessica pushed away her unease. The man had only been in the country for three weeks, according to his letter, obviously he hadn't had time to furnish yet, what with all his secretarial problems and his continued absences from his office. She wondered cynically how many other secretarial agencies had weathered his insults. If Wright-Waverly hadn't been his first choice, perhaps she could use it as a lever . . . he certainly wouldn't get a better service anywhere else.

She walked through the third door. Civilisation at last! A desk, obviously in use, two chairs, a few books on the bookshelf, and a small computer terminal, winking a message at her. She walked across the thick acid green carpet with a sigh. It seemed Mr Martin Gibson wasn't even going to bother to meet his latest secretary.

Obeying the instructions on the screen Jessica pressed a combination of buttons on the keyboard which was swivelled towards her. Expecting a screed of instructions to hit the screen she was surprised to see a single line write itself before her eyes.

Welcome to my parlour

The moving finger paused and Jessica frowned. Was that it? Had she pressed the wrong keys? No, the little green blip was moving on . . . a comma and another word. Jessica straightened with a choked cry, backing away in disbelief.

Welcome to my parlour,
Love.

She heard a soft click behind her and jerked around. Matthew Grieve was leaning against the door, swinging a key from an indolent hand. He was smiling.

'I knew you wouldn't be able to resist the chance to put an arrogant male in his place. Sit down, *Love*, before you fall down.'

Jessica clutched at the desk behind her. M. G.

Martin Gibson. Matthew Grieve. Why hadn't it occurred to her? Because she had been too busy shoring up her courage with wishful thinking.

'How did you . . .?' She stopped herself just in time, gathering her scattered wits. Relax. Breathe. Relax. But her pulse defied control. It was his smile that scared her. A gloating, complacent smile, not the viciously angry one of the other night.

'I hired a detective. You're an elusive woman, Jessica Anne Wright. But, unfortunately for you, not elusive enough.'

'You had me *investigated*!' Jessica croaked with mingled fear and outrage.

'You should have given the taxi driver a better story. All I had to do was pile on a few more hearts and flowers. He was a sucker for a happy ending. From there it was purely a matter of routine for my investigator. I know everything about you, Love, from the moment you were born. I know how much money you have in the bank, I know all about your business, I know all about your private life. I know what your favourite food is, I know what you sleep in, I even know what brand of perfume you use.'

Icy fingers were sliding down Jessica's spine as she listened to his calm, slow recitation. She felt naked, exposed before a stranger. He knew the intimate details of her life, but what did she knew about him? Nothing.

His face was harder than she remembered it, bones more exposed. His mouth was thin, his smile trembling on the verge of a sneer, the cynicism even more prominent than it had been that night in Devon.

Jessica pushed herself fully upright, determined not to let him have his victory so easily. With her high heels she could match him in height, she could also match him in defiant anger.

'Am I supposed to be frightened by your stand-over

tactics? Is this how you got rid of the secretaries I sent you, by hectoring and bullying? Well, I don't scare so easily, Mr Gibson!' She used his false name deliberately.

'I should be disappointed if you did, Love,' he said with soft menace. 'Healthy opposition always stimulates my competitive instincts. And the name is Grieve, as well you know, Love.'

'Will you stop calling me that!' The way he curled his tongue around the *l* and lingered on the vowel gave her the creeps.

'Does it disturb you?' He came towards her and she hastily moved away from the desk. He gave a soft laugh and leant on the edge she had clutched so frantically. 'Nerves getting a bit raw?'

'Look, Mr Grieve, I don't know what all this is about but I'm a busy woman. I don't have time to play incomprehensible games.' She lifted her chin and gave him a hard, haughty stare. He merely jingled the keys in his hands mockingly.

'Oh no, Jessica. Not three times. You don't talk your way out of it this time. I don't unlock that door until you've made a full confession.'

She felt a hot surge of temper that momentarily eclipsed her trepidation. 'You can't *make* me do anything. This—idiocy—has gone far enough. Now give me the key!' With each word she felt a return of confidence. He wasn't making any physical threats. She sensed a difference in him, a passivity that encouraged her at the same time as it irritated her.

'Very impressive.' The dark eyes gleamed at her defiant stance. 'No wonder they call you the Amazon. Did you know that's what some of your clients call you . . . so my informant at Spiron Construction tells me. Though I can personally attest to one major dissimilarity between you and those legendary females.' He was looking at her breasts, reminding her of how she had allowed him to touch them under that low-cut black gown on *that* night.

'*Give me the key!*' she ordered furiously, as if by willpower alone she could make him obey.

The lean shoulders moved under the faultlessly cut grey suit as he slid the key into the breast pocket of his cream shirt. 'Come and get it,' he invited, with a smile. If she hadn't loathed him so much she might have thought that the smile made him an extremely attractive man. As it was it made him all the more repellent.

Jessica ignored the challenge. Instead she picked up the push-button telephone from the desk and punched in the Agency's number. Matthew Grieve allowed the tone to ring once before he casually reached down and ripped the cord from the wall connection.

'What did you do that for?' Jessica snapped, the act of vandalism oddly disturbing. If he was prone to wanton destruction at whim what had he in mind for her? 'Don't you know it's illegal to tamper with telephones in this country?'

'Surely a little thing like illegality doesn't worry you? You, a common little thief!'

'I don't know what you're talking about,' she said coldly, trying to control her temper. He was taunting her deliberately with that casual offensiveness . . . all smiles and soft challenges.

'Well, Jessica, what happens now? You can't jump out the window. There's no one else here to appeal to. What are you going to do? What *can* you do?'

Jessica had never felt so helpless, or so indecisive. She flinched when Matthew Grieve rose slowly to his feet, so that the two pairs of brown eyes were on a level.

'There is one way. I'm surprised you haven't tried it before now. I know you have the aptitude.' He reached out and brushed his fingers across the centre of her right breast, a searing contact that exploded light into Jessica's brain. My God. Sex! He was suggesting she use sex to bargain for her freedom! So that's the form he intended his revenge to take.

Jessica reacted with characteristic speed to the insult, not thinking, just instinctively reacting with a tried and true technique. But when she reached for him, to her complete astonishment he wasn't there. He had moved, changing his point of balance, pulling her further into her movement, sweeping her bodily off the floor in a circular motion and wheeling her over his hip with a flick of his loins. As she lay gasping on her back, trying to take in what had happened, Matthew Grieve dropped down on top of her, his chest pressing down on hers, his hips resting on the carpet. As she moved to roll away he grabbed her left wrist in his left hand and pushed her arm flat on the floor, forcing her elbow to bend at a right angle. At the same time his right arm slid under her left shoulder and clasped his own left wrist. A slight clockwise turn of his right wrist and forearm forced her shoulder to lift and she gasped at the pain from her trapped arm.

'Submit?'

Jessica looked into the dark brown eyes only inches away from her own. There was a deep, searing satisfaction in their murky depths, a savage, relentless passion unmasked. *This* was what he had wanted. This . . . *physical* subjugation, the bodily affirmation of his male superiority.

She was trapped in a web of his making.

Jessica tried to roll him off her chest, knowing that her feeble effort was ineffective against this particular arm-lock.

'Submit,' he ordered savagely, turning his hand again, forcing her shoulder even higher, his eyes avid on her face as he watched the knowledge growing on her face, the realisation that she was utterly helpless.

He was defeating her at her own sport, grinding her pride into the green carpet along with her body.

She swore at him weakly as the pain in her arm intensified. He was increasing the pressure slowly, relentlessly, and she was helplessly aware that he was in deadly earnest. He meant to have her admission of defeat, even if it meant dislocating her shoulder or breaking her arm. *As soon as a lock applied against you commences to take effect you must submit.* The words from the judo manual had been drummed into her over the years but never had she felt so stubbornly determined to defy them. Perhaps she would faint from the pain and escape into unconsciousness? Matthew Grieve would probably wait until she woke up and do the same thing all over again. It wouldn't change the bitter fact that he had beaten her.

'Submit, Jessica?' he whispered with bloodthirsty relish. 'You know you'll have to sometime. Such a little word, Love. Say it.'

She tried to close her ears to his triumph. Her head was pounding as if it was going to explode.

'Let me up!' she spat at him with another curse, gritting her teeth against her rage.

'When you say the word. At least I gave you a chance, lady. At least you weren't half-asleep and suffering from jetlag. At least I allowed you the courtesy of making the first move. And still you lost. A brown belt, aren't you? So am I.'

She glared at him in silent loathing. She had known, the instant he applied the lock, that he was as good as, or better, than she. But he *had* taken her by surprise, just as she had done to him. In an equal bout either of them might win. She went cold at the mere thought of what could have happened in Devon if he had been prepared . . . she had risked far more than she knew.

'We can lie here all day, if necessary. I have no objections,' he said maliciously and suddenly another dimension was added to her humiliation. He hadn't moved but he had managed to emphasise the vulnerability of her position. Her unbuttoned jacket was caught beneath her, her breasts crushed by the slanting weight of his chest. Her sleek skirt had ridden up around her thighs and her other hand was trapped against the floor by the hard ridge of his hipbone.

'All right.' She closed her eyes so that she wouldn't see the gloating look on his face at her capitulation.

'All right what?'

'All right, you can let me up.'

'That's not enough, Jessica. And open your eyes.'

She obeyed because she had no choice. But she wasn't going to pretend repentance. Her eyes flamed defiance.

'I submit,' she flung at him as if the words were a challenge rather than a defeat.

His head jerked up and for an instant he increased the pressure on her shoulder until she gave a half-choked cry of agony. 'You need a few lessons in humility, Jessica Wright.'

'Whose going to teach me, you!' she was scornful, despite the fact that the pain had made her breathless. 'Grace in defeat? Don't make me laugh!'

'I could very easily break your arm.'

'Go to hell!'

An incredible flash of humour passed over his face. 'I've already been there, I didn't like it. If I have to go again, I'll take company.' He slanted a wolfish smile at her, so that she was in no doubt of who he would drag down with him.

'I'd have thought you'd feel very much at home there.'

'Don't push your luck, Jessica.'

'Then let me up, I said what you wanted me to. Now let me up.'

'You broke into my house in Devon, and stole some letters.'

Jessica glared at him, tight-lipped. He could drag her to hell and back but she wasn't conceding him another word. Implicit in the statement was a certain knowledge and she wasn't going to give him the satisfaction of confirming it.

Suddenly she was free. Matthew Grieve unpeeled his body from hers with supple ease and extended a hand down to her. Contemptuously she struck it away, ignoring his hiss of temper, and scrambled to her feet, trying to put her clothes into some kind of order.

'Unlock the door,' she demanded.

His face tightened. He walked around the desk and sat down in the swivel chair. 'Sit down.' When she hesitated his voice flicked like a whip. 'Sit down, Jessica, or it's going to be a very long day for both of us.'

Matthew watched Jessica slowly obey, and waited for the hot thrust of victory. It didn't come. With savage frustration he realised that even in defeat she was defying him. Her attitude was unrepentant. There was no fear and guilt on her pale face, only fury at her own helplessness and a contempt that bit deeply into his pride. Her strength of will inspired in him, not admiration, but a greedy desire to hurt and to go on hurting until he wiped away that look of contempt and replaced it with one of respect.

What in the hell gave her the right to sit there in judgment of him? She and her brother had chosen to believe the worst of him, why should he disillusion her? Why should he attempt to justify himself? His anger whipped into fury. By her deliberate interference this arrogant woman had exposed his private agonies to the world; destroyed his hopes of ending a farcical marriage in a reasonably civilised manner. Very well, he thought bitterly, if she saw him as a cruel and callous monster that was what he would be, and in the process he would teach her the consequences of meddling in other people's business!

A slight change in scenario was all that was needed, and, fortuitously, the means were at hand. Instead of merely mental suffering, he'd cause her a bit of physical discomfort too . . . remove the fight to home ground. His anticipation had a sweet-sharp pleasure to it that was almost sexual. Lisa had been beneath contempt but this woman . . . by her very nature she was a challenge to him and when had he ever backed away from a challenge?

He fingered the piece of paper in front of him. 'I know all about your visit to England eighteen months ago. *All* the details. Would you like to check?'

Silently he handed her a piece of paper. His eyes were black and shiny as river stones, and just about as warm.

She took it slowly and looked down at it, trying to keep him in the periphery of her vision. It was a confidential telex, a detailed report on her movements in England eighteen months ago. There were receipt numbers for the purchase of one black evening gown and gloves, and a black woollen balaclava, the hire of costume jewellery. There was also information from a rental car agency—one night's car hire and the mileage involved. The report was signed 'Stormont Security' and dated five days ago. So only since seeing her here had Matthew Grieve been able to pick up the threads of that night.

'It's not a crime to visit one's relatives, or to buy clothes in another country.' She threw the paper scornfully down.

He took her dismissal of his evidence calmly. He rose with controlled ease and crossed over to a painting on the wall. He swung it back to reveal a safe.

Jessica couldn't help the leap of her pulses. His head

snapped around and caught the sudden flush on her face.

'Bring back memories of past triumphs, Love?'

'Don't call me that!' Jessica ordered automatically as she watched him open it and lift out a black metal box. He carried it back to the desk and unlocked it. Jessica waited in an agony of suspense as he opened the lid, aware that he was prolonging this moment of discovery deliberately.

'I had this air-freighted over, just for you.' Carefully he lifted out a clear perspex cube. Inside was a glass, smudged with faint white marks. 'Recognise it?'

Oh God! She remembered, with merciless clarity, stripping off her glove to pull back his eyelid. She hadn't replaced it.

'Isn't forensic science a marvellous thing?' he said, turning the cube in his hands before carefully replacing it. 'They've even invented a laser which can uncover "invisible" prints on damp surfaces—like the moist side of a glass.'

Under her crumpled armour Jessica's body was dissolving to jelly. It all sounded so horribly official. If he *had* reported it to the police why hadn't anything got into print? Was he bluffing? Jessica looking down at her betraying hands, clenched in her lap.

'I know they're yours,' he told her, enjoying the small, trapped movement of her head. 'My investigators were very thorough.'

His taunt had her come out fighting. 'I don't believe you can use that as proof. The police would never have let you take away a piece of vital evidence like that!'

'Not officially, no. But I have friends in very high places——' Calmly he extracted a sheaf of black and white photographs and handed them to her. They were close-ups of the prints on the glass, and there were file numbers printed on the corner of each

photograph. 'I didn't make a *formal* complaint because
I couldn't find anything missing. But I made certain
. . . contingency plans just in case. In my business it
pays to be as underhanded as the next man . . . or
woman. When I finally did find out, I was fully aware
of my position . . . I had no way of proving those
letters were fakes, faking *innocence*. And if ever I
found you I had no interest in letting the law impose
its petty trespass penalties on you . . . oh yes, I'm well
aware of English law in that respect. That was what
you were banking on, wasn't it? So I mentioned to my
friends about the jewellery, unofficially of course, since
it was uninsured and there was no question of a
fraudulent claim, and since there was the embarrassing
possibility my wife might have appropriated it. They
were *very* understanding.'

'Jewellery?' Jessica's confusion showed in her wide,
hazel eyes.

'Ten thousand pound's worth. Don't tell me you
didn't see it in the safe?'

'I didn't take any jewellery!'

'Then who did? It disappeared that night.'

'I didn't touch it I tell you. I only took the damned
letters! I didn't——' she broke off with an angry
exclamation, realising this had been another of his
intricately woven webs.

'Quite so. Thank you for those revealing words.
Don't look so upset, Jessica, confession is good for the
soul.'

'You tricked me! You're lying about the jewellery!'

'I admit it took a certain amount of foresight on my
part. After all, I wasn't sure that this——' he indicated
her presence with a wave of his hand '—would ever
happen. But now it has, and I'm confident that,
should you prove unco-operative in certain matters,
the "missing" jewellery will turn up here, in your
possession.'

'No! You can't set me up, I won't let you!' Jessica cried passionately.

'Believe me, it would be very simple to arrange.'

'You wouldn't . . . not even you! . . . you *couldn't*!'

'Oh, Jessica, you make one mistake after another,' he warned with chilling softness. 'I can do anything I want with you.' With each word he spoke, his anger renewed itself, his towering confidence such that Jessica felt the bile rise in her throat. 'Were you so naïve as to think that I would kiss goodbye to several hundred thousand pounds without wanting to know *how* and *why* and *who*? I didn't succeed in finding out then, but I have now. And I shall use that knowledge in any way I choose. You cost me a lot of money. You *owe* me. Nobody welches on a debt to Matthew Grieve. Even if I hadn't found you for five years, or ten or twenty, I still would have made you pay.'

'*I* didn't take your money. Your wife——'

'My *wife*,' he made the word a harsh curse, 'was a bitch and a whore; greedy and shrewish, and hard as nails when it came to money. But she was a coward, an opportunist—she would never have taken those letters herself. She knew me too well. *You* made it easy for her.'

'I didn't do it for her. If you know so much about me and Carl then you know why I did it. If you had had any compassion——'

'Compassion!' he grated contemptuously. 'How much compassion did you have for me? Did you think that because I was wealthy I wasn't entitled to common human decency? Did my money make me unfit for the protection of the law? You set yourself up as judge and jury and carried out the sentence without even seeing me.'

Every word was a stab to the heart. He was voicing every doubt she had ever had about what she had done. If he knew that she agreed with any part of what he said, he would crush her mercilessly.

'Carl was——'

'Carl was an adulterer. He slept with my wife. God knows she was free enough with her favours, but don't tell me your precious stepbrother was blameless. He was an eager and inventive lover, Lisa had the grace to fling in my face.' He pounced on Jessica's wince of shocked disgust. 'Oh yes, she admitted it ... after the final decree was granted. Gave me all the intimate details. He knew exactly what he was doing, he just didn't have the guts to take the consequences like a man.'

She was shocked, aware of additional undercurrents that she couldn't interpret. That Lisa had taunted her husband with her infidelity was sickening. 'All right, so what Carl did was wrong. But he was distraught. You and your wife were going to hurt the two people most dear to him in the world.'

'He should have thought of that before.'

'But he didn't, he was blindly unhappy, he——'

'He had no sympathy for me, why should I have any for him?'

Jessica wavered. 'Lisa said——'

'Oh, I can guess what she *said*.' His voice was thick with loathing. 'And of course you and your brother believed every word. How could anyone so beautiful tell a lie? I was so much better fitted to be the villain, wasn't I?'

Jessica stumbled to her feet, dismayed by the bitter sneering words, and the hurt they implied. 'I never met your ... ex-wife. I only know what Carl told me. How was I to know——'

He cut her off with an oath. The fleeting instant of pity he had glimpsed causing a violent spasm of rejection. How dare she pity him! He wanted her to fight, not give in; to resist, to give him something to

smash. *Fight, damn you.* 'I can still destroy him ..
and you,' he said viciously. 'Even if the theft case is
thrown out of court it will still have dragged out all the
dirty little secrets you're so anxious to hide.' Eyes
impaling her he reached into the top drawer of his
desk and produced a tape-recorder, still running. He
laughed harshly at her expression.

'Out of your own mouth you condemn yourself.
And, after editing, it could be even more damning.
Framing you will be like taking candy from a baby.'

Jessica's reasoning processes went into suspended
animation. She was trapped back in her nightmare.
Wildly she wondered whether she could make a
sweeping grab for that damning evidence, smash the
glass and rip out the tape. Then she saw the waiting,
wanting look on his face and realised that he hadn't yet
worked out that violent desire he had to hurt her.

'Why? Why are you doing this?' she whispered. 'To
go to all this trouble after so long.'

'Oh, it was no trouble, I assure you,' he drawled,
delighted to reveal just how capricious fate had been.
'These offices, for example, are intended as the
headquarters of a new Australasian development
company I'm launching. Just doing my bit for the
Closer Economic Relationship that our two
Governments are so committed to promoting.
Discovering you was an unexpected bonus. Simply
because I hadn't forgotten you, doesn't mean that I've
spent all these months brooding. That would have
been an unproductive waste of effort.'

'And revenge. Isn't that unproductive? What profit
is there in what you're threatening to do to me?'
Jessica's voice trembled on the edge of breaking.

'Revenge? You misunderstand me, Jessica.' He
smiled cruelly. 'At the moment my threats are just
that—threats. I don't want to carry them out any
more than you want me to. In fact it's just what I

want to avoid. I don't want revenge, I want *reparation*.'

'Reparation?' Jessica was disbelieving. 'You mean . . . money?'

He named a sum that took away what little breath she had left. She laughed in his face, convinced this was another turn of the mental screw.

'I don't have anything like that kind of money.'

'I know. So you'll have to earn it.'

'Where would I earn that kind of money?' she asked hoarsely, realising from his expression that he was serious. And that this was the demand that all the others had been leading up to.

'From me. In kind.'

'*What!*' Jessica felt the whole world was collapsing in on itself in madness. Fear tightened an iron band around her chest. There was an implacable purpose on the lean, hard face confronting her that told her he was not going to be swayed by pleas for mercy—though he might enjoy listening to her beg.

'I have a job for you, one that'll settle the debt.' He saw her sudden suspicion. 'Oh, nothing criminal, *Love*, but certainly dishonest enough to warm the cockles of your crooked little heart.'

Whatever it was, Jessica wanted no part of it. 'You can't make me——'

'I can and I will,' he promised brutally. 'I can break you into little pieces. I have the money and the power, and the influence to do it. I can even destroy your business—a court case, a little word here, and rumour there. You're about to invest a sizeable proportion of your capital in a computer, financially you're very vulnerable.'

Jessica could sit no longer. She rose in bitter rage. 'You bastard! That's blackmail.'

His eyes glittered with satisfaction. 'Ironclad, Love. You owe me. Pay up or give up . . . *everything*.' He sat back, cool now that she was trembling visibly with helpless frustration. Her eyes caught the light from the wide, tinted windows behind him and reflected a golden, blazing fire. Her strong, lithe body was also ablaze, blood roaring through her veins in a way that made her feel faint with the need for action. But there was none she could take. She was utterly trapped and he knew it.

The last vestiges of sympathy she had felt for him were banished by a choking surge of fury and contempt. Revenge—for all it was profitless, at least it was a red-blooded human instinct, an excuse of a sort for cruelty. But this . . . this merciless obsession with reparation . . .! Money. It *was* only the money he cared about, after all, and power.

'No wonder your wife wanted to escape from you; no wonder you couldn't satisfy her! You couldn't satisfy any woman!' she raged at him wildly. 'There's nothing inside you, just empty space. Other people are just things to use, possessions to buy and sell. I'm glad. *I'm glad* that I took those letters! I'd do it again, if I got the chance. You deserve every damned thing you get!'

'I'm glad you agree with me,' he said, with a soft, stony blankness. 'Because for the next month I've got *you*. Exclusive use of. You're going to come to Sydney with me.'

Jessica felt wrung out by her explosion. She simply stared at him.

'You see, I need a temporary mistress.' He watched with grim humour as she sank bonelessly back into her seat, flushing with outraged shock. 'Calm yourself, Jessica, I didn't mean it literally. I want you to act the part. You're very good at lying and deception, it shouldn't be too difficult for you.'

'You think I . . . you're crazy,' Jessica croaked as absurdity piled on absurdity.

He ignored her, coolly returning the box containing the glass to the safe, along with the cassette tape and the slim but shattering detective file. He stood, half-turned to the window, displaying a tough, unrevealing profile to Jessica's incredulous gaze. The high jut of his cheekbone emphasised the hollow below it and the tight line of his mouth. He spoke in a clipped, controlled manner that yet hinted at the restraint he was exercising. Jessica sensed once more the violence in him and knew that this was what had made him such a successful businessman, the ability to channel all the dark, driving forces within him to a single purpose. Nothing would sway him. Oh, he might be sidetracked for a while, briefly distracted, but ultimately he would achieve whatever he set out to achieve.

'Shortly I'm going to be involved in a very delicate business negotiation involving millions of dollars—a merger, between my own computer company and one of equal stature. I am acquainted only slightly with the owner of the other company, but I do know that he demands the utmost probity in those with whom he deals. He is coming to stay at my home in Sydney, to "get to know me" before he makes a final decision.'

'And you want to drag me along as your so-called mistress?' Jessica demanded. 'What do you want to do . . . sabotage the deal?'

He turned, one eyebrow raised derisively. 'Don't even think the word, Jessica. I'm two steps ahead of you all the way. No, Kent Farrow may be conservative, but he wouldn't be in the electronics industry if he was *that* old-fashioned. I'm a single man with normal appetites. It would be unusual, even suspicious, at my age if I didn't have a woman in my life.'

'And you don't?' Jessica cut in, wondering.

'I do. Several in fact.' Cynicism tugged at his

mouth. 'None whom I trust. If I made them the offer I'm making you, I've no doubts I'd be in court on breach of promise within a week of signing the contract with Farrow.'

The note of contempt in his voice was real and chilling. Was there any woman he trusted? What about his mother? Jessica struggled to deny herself the least curiosity.

'Charming women you know,' she said sarcastically.

'Oh yes, you're all as charming as vipers. Fortunately I have a forked stick to deal with you,' he reminded her crushingly. 'To continue. Farrow's wife, another viper, is threatening to jeopardise everything with her wandering eye. If she continues to be ... indiscreet ... in expressing her interest in me her husband is bound to notice—particularly if we're all living in the same house. I need a buffer. I want to make it very clear to this woman that I am not interested, but I cannot openly insult her. I cannot afford to make an enemy of her until Farrow has signed on the dotted line. I have already told them that I am involved with an intelligent ... amusing ... and beautiful woman.' His sarcastic emphasis sent a quiver down Jessica's nerves. So he thought she was beautiful? She dredged up an expression of insult.

'And what if I blow the gaff? Tell this man what is going on ... I can blackmail too, you know.'

'I can always make another million, but your stepbrother will never practice medicine again, and your sister-in-law may have another mental breakdown. And you, Jessica, you will be bankrupt.' He watched her sustain each icy blow. 'You will obey me ... in this and in everything else. And if you satisfy me, when my business is concluded you'll have everything that is in that safe in your hands. You will have paid your debt in full.'

'How do I know that?' she asked thickly, disgusted

at her own weak desire to burst into tears and throw herself on his non-existent mercy.

He smiled. 'You'll have to trust me.'

'I wouldn't trust you as far as I could throw you,' she said fiercely.

'The feeling is entirely mutual, but for what it's worth you have my word of honour.'

Honour! What did he know about the word? On the other hand he gave her little choice. He wasn't the kind of man to make empty threats. Anyone with the slightest grain of compassion could never have made such threats in the first place. Could she perhaps confess that she was underqualified for the position he was forcing her into? God no, that would be another weapon for him. He would probably enjoy the irony of parading a virgin as his mistress.

'I'm not an actress, you know. I wouldn't be able to hide the fact that I can't stand to be near you,' she said, voicing the doubt in a mist of evasion.

'Really? You did well enough that night in Devon . . . convincing me you were stricken with a consuming lust for my flesh.'

'It was all I could do not to be sick!'

Something flared in the darkness of his eyes. 'Then you really are Oscar material,' he said softly, 'because all my male instincts told me otherwise, and my instincts are usually right.'

The gleam in his black eyes should have prepared her, but she registered it a fraction of a second too late. They were almost of a height but Jessica discovered that with his arms clamped about her she felt small and weak. She tried to struggle but he lifted a hand, gripping her neck painfully, lowering his mouth to bite at her closed lips.

She clenched her teeth and tried to bring her knee up between his legs but he wrenched her around, pushing her back against the sharp angle of the desk.

Her breasts were tight against his hard chest, her hips pressed into his by the protruding edge of the desk, high-heeled shoes trapped between his feet. He held her too closely for her to get a proper grip on him. She jerked her head back, cursing him for the devil he was, her lips bruised by his teeth, suddenly conscious of the upsurge of heat trapped between their two bodies. She had been held this closely by a man before, but never had she been so conscious of the erotic potential of this living bondage. The animal appeal she had recognised in him once before was suddenly a real threat. Something long concealed within her began to beat into awareness, sapping her will to resist.

'Am I hurting you?' he grated against her savaged mouth. 'So now you know that I can bite too, Jessica. You're not going to get your fangs into me this time.' Reminding her brutally of how she had escaped him at the party.

'No!' she arched against the iron hand at her nape, refusing to respond to the violence in him, to satisfy his sexual curiosity.

'Yes.' His mouth was on hers again. His arm was like a steel coil around her waist, all of him was hard except his mouth; that was soft, and moist and far more dangerous than anything that had come before.

Her breath was constricted by the press of his cheek against her nose and Jessica tried desperately to suck in oxygen through her mouth. It was her undoing. Instead she found herself absorbing his male breath, sustaining her life force from his lungs. His mouth shifted, settled, feeding greedily on her tentative response. His tongue burned its way into the dark cavern of her mouth, she felt it everywhere, deep, penetrating, sucking away her resistance . . . meeting, fighting with hers, drawing her back into his mouth, holding her there, allowing her to savour the alien taste of him.

Still her body refused to succumb, fighting off the inevitability of desire at the same time as her mouth accepted it. All conscious thought had stopped. She was kissing him back without even realising it, roused to the same aggressive passion that she had shown him once before. But this time it was a totally physical response, rather than angry desire to teach him a lesson. He felt it. Felt the beginnings of involuntary response in her body, the conflict between passion and reason that suddenly had her twisting in panic, forgetting all her training in the need to escape the consequences of her self-betrayal.

This time he let her succeed in breaking free and they glared at each other for a moment, tension crackling in the air.

'No Oscar this year, Love,' he jeered. 'A most unconvincing display of revulsion.' But Jessica glimpsed the unappeased hunger in the black eyes that gave her a tiny measure of satisfaction in the midst of her horrified embarrassment. So he, too, had been jolted. He was not quite as implacably cool as he pretended to be.

'You——' the word came thickly between her swollen lips as she sought for a strong enough insult, but he beat her to it once again.

'You needn't worry that I'll try and make fiction fact, I never go to bed with thieves. You never know whether your wallet is still going to be there in the morning. Besides, as snakes go, I think you might be of the boa constrictor variety ... if I let you, you'd devour me whole.'

Jessica hated him for that last cruelty. She writhed in self-disgust to think that he had seen how close she had come to losing her self-control in that sudden surge of erotic craving. If he had kept on kissing her, pushing her to meet his sexual challenge, she might have actually ... God, he had almost succeeded in making her as animalistic as himself! Something about him appealed to the basest urges of her nature, and that frightened her much more than his threats to bankrupt her, or drag her through the courts. 'All right, Jessica, you can go now, you'll be hearing from me.' He sat down in his chair without looking at her, drawing the computer keyboard towards himself. 'You'd better get your affairs in order, I want to leave at the end of the week—NO arguments!' as she attempted a feeble sound.

'I was only going to ask you to unlock the door so that I can get as far away from you as possible.' She glared at his downbent head.

He lifted an expression of diabolical laughter. 'Not too far I trust, Jessica. Remember, I have someone watching every move you make. And the door was never locked. Interesting, isn't it, how often your assumptions about me affect the power of your reasoning? You never actually saw me lock it, did you? Poor Jessica, "cabin'd, cribb'd and confin'd" by your own mistakes.'

Jessica ripped the door open and raged out into the corridor, followed by the hated sound of his mocking laughter. That last blow had been the most devastating of them all, completely destroying the last shreds of composure. Stupid, stupid, stupid! He was all bluff. She would be boiled in oil before she ever moved an inch with him!

CHAPTER SIX

'CHAMPAGNE?' the stewardess enquired and Jessica opened her mouth to refuse politely. It would never do to give Matthew Grieve the impression that she was *enjoying* her first experience of first class air travel.

'The lady will have orange juice. A whisky and soda on the rocks for me, please.'

'Yes, of course, sir.' With a warm smile the woman busied herself at the trolley in the aisle while Jessica glared at the man in the seat beside her.

'How dare you tell her that?' she whispered angrily. 'I can have whatever I want. It's free isn't it? It's not going to cost you anything!'

'Nothing is ever free.' His attention barely shifted from the closely typed papers in front of him. They had absorbed his entire attention since leaving Auckland. Jessica had fumed silently out the window at her elbow, the empty blue sky her only audience.

'Besides, *darling*,' he added with a mocking drawl as he accepted his drink, 'you know that you have no head for alcohol, I don't want to have to carry you off the plane.'

Jessica tried to ignore the stewardess' amusement as she moved away. 'What makes you think I can't hold my drink?' she demanded aggressively.

He sipped his drink and gave her a cool, knowing look. Jessica's bosom swelled with outrage.

'Your slimy detective, I suppose, pawing through my life with his grubby little magnifying glass! Well, your impeccable source slipped up, then. I don't drink much because I *choose* not to, not because I can't.'

'And that's so important to you, isn't it, Jessica, to

do as you *choose*.' He invested her name with a deep, sardonic sibilance that taunted her with her present predicament. She was here, now, because he had taken away her ability to choose. One by one he had stopped up all the avenues of escape. He had kindly allowed her a day or two to wriggle on his hook before he had casually reeled her in. He had gone behind her back to Jill, bearing some cock-and-bull story about needing a top-flight secretary with basic Japanese and holding out the prospect of further, lucrative employment contracts if the Agency could satisfy him on this occasion. He had discussed it with Jessica, he told Jill, but she was loath to take on such a plum job herself and leave her partner to cope on her own yet again.

Consequently Jessica had found herself almost hustled off the premises.

And Matthew had certainly wasted no time consolidating his hold over Jessica. He issued orders ranging from what she was to tell her friends, to what she was to wear.

'Don't pack anything casual or tailored,' he had said, not tempering the demand with politeness. 'You're my mistress, not my secretary, you don't have to wear anything practical. Plenty of leg and plenty of cleavage.'

'Should I chew gum and dye my hair the colour of brass, too?' Jessica had snapped, instantly rearranging her suitcase in her mind. She would take everything casual and tailored that she had. So busy was she planning her minor revenge that she didn't see the cynical look of dark-eyed assessment he gave her at her lack of further argument. He was beginning to realise that keeping one step ahead of his defiant captive was going to be even more of a challenge than he had anticipated.

When the stewardess came back to serve their brunch Jessica quickly held out her wine glass to be filled. She took a long swallow, daring him to take it off her.

'Enjoy your petty victory, Jessica,' he murmured, apparently undisturbed. 'As long as I have your obedience on major issues, I can tolerate your minor rebellions.'

Obedience. How he loved to toss words like that around. Obey. Permit. Allow. Every now and then he applied a deliberate twitch of the reins.

'I'm not a windup doll. Don't think that, just because you've got me this far, that you can control my every thought.'

'As long as I command your body, I don't give a damn for your soul.'

Jessica's appetite deserted her as she watched him dine with relish on lamb cutlets and asparagus. When he mentioned her body, casually like that, she felt her insides tense. If he knew that it wasn't the thought of her public role that made her nervous, but her private reactions to him ... oh no, he must never discover that!

In fact the public side of things didn't daunt her at all. She would be herself and if that wasn't good enough, too bad. People were free to assume what they liked, and usually did according to their own morality. Jessica was a virgin but she wasn't a prude, nor was she a slave to conformity. These days no one thought twice about people living together.

Nor was she worried about future complications. When and if she got married it would be to an intelligent man who didn't expect a virgin unsullied *as of right*. She didn't look on her virginity as a priceless gift to be hoarded as a dowry. But she did value her body, and respect it. Sex without love held no temptations for her.

That clear, Jessica wondered why the body she

valued so much was so unpredictable around a man she professed to hate and despise. She was very aware of him, and prey to all kinds of uncertainties that had never bothered her before. What if he decided after all to make fiction fact? She hastily shoved that one away. Her doubts were probably only resulting from a mild attack of the Stockholm Syndrome—the theory that captives were sometimes attracted to their captors as a subconscious form of self-defence.

'What about these people I'm supposed to be fooling with this charade?' she demanded, shaking off her introspection. 'Hadn't you better tell me about them?'

'Kent and Kristin Farrow. They live in Melbourne. His firm is called Computronics.' Matthew was deliberately terse, unwilling to fall into the trap of normal conversation. He needed to maintain the distance between them, a safety margin. Already he had taken this thing much further than he had originally intended. She had been a dehumanised super-bitch for so long in his mind that the living, breathing, more complex reality was proving difficult, and disturbing, to assimilate.

'And what about us? What have you told them about us?'

'A slightly censored version of the truth. We met eighteen months ago in England and recently renewed our fascinating acquaintanceship at a party in Auckland, at which time you decided that you weren't going to let me slip through your fingers a second time.'

'You make it sound as if I'm the one doing the running?'

'You are.'

His smug reply made Jessica grind her teeth. Being thought a man's mistress was one thing, but her pride rejected the idea that she was to be the pursuer. She wouldn't cross the street for Matthew Grieve, let alone run after him!

'God I hate you,' was all she permitted herself to say through tight lips. She was unprepared for the way that he turned on her, eyes smouldering with menace. The pupils were piercingly narrow pinpoints, but the irises were such a dark bistre that they seemed as sooty as the centres.

'Hate away, for all the good it'll do you. But in public you'll be my lover. You'll hang on my words, follow me with your hungry eyes. You'll want me, desire me, *need* me.'

Jessica shrank from the threat in the lean body, from the darkly erotic litany. Imagine being so in his thrall that she would do that; imagine wanting him, desiring that grimly narrowed mouth sliding over her skin, needing that strong sinuous body pressing over hers. A woman would have to be mad! His passion would probably be as violent as his temper. He would insist on taking control, on squeezing every last drop of pleasure from his lovemaking; he would be voracious, fierce, bold, and quite possibly wildly inventive.

Jessica went scarlet at the thought, appalled by the trend of her thoughts. Such carnality was foreign to her.

'Like hell I will,' she blazed at him.

'Not only that, but you will hit the roof in spectacular style if I so much as *look* at another woman while in your company.'

'Hah!' was all the comeback Jessica could manage, thinking that if a woman was jealously involved with Matthew Grieve she was signing her own ticket to the madhouse. *He* would never be owned by anyone. She pondered that thought for the rest of the flight.

With ease of long practice Matthew whisked her through Customs and Immigration at Sydney airport, commandeering her passport afterwards with a brief: 'You won't be needing that for a while.' Jessica took one look at his face and decided against making a scene. She did, however, protest when he firmly steered her outside to a waiting limousine.

'But what about our luggage?'

'That's being sent on. Get in, Jessica. I have an appointment in an hour and I want to go home first and collect some papers.'

'*When* is it going to be sent on?' Jessica stood her ground as a young man in a uniform got out of the driver's seat and opened the rear door. First her passport, now this.

'Thank you, Mike.' Matthew nodded to the young man, who got back behind the wheel. 'I don't have the time to hang around airports waiting for baggage. Why did you think I told you to pack a few things in your flight bag? Get *in*, Jessica.'

She went, reluctantly. She had one change of clothes and a nightie and spongebag in the Qantas bag—as per *order*. Although it went against the grain to trust him, he was the more experienced traveller of the two and what he said made sense.

Jessica had not been in Sydney for ten years, so she looked with interest out of the tinted windows as the car purred through the suburbs of the city. What kind of house would he have—a vintage mansion or an expensive apartment in the city? She couldn't even guess. She didn't know whether his wealth was inherited, or whether he had clawed his way up from the gutter ... he had the patina of ruthlessness that suggested the latter. Did he have a family? Would she be expected to act the whore in front of a sister or brother ... or, God forbid, his mother!

'Where do you live? Where are your offices?' She had to repeat herself before he looked at her, a distant expression on his face that told her his thoughts had been far away.

'I live in Paddington and I have offices in Pitt Street. I'm thirty-five. I have all my own teeth. I sleep in the raw. I have all the normal male appetites.'

And then some, thought Jessica, wary of his flat, emotionless delivery. 'OK, OK, I just thought I'd ask.'

'If you're looking for weaknesses, don't bother, I haven't got any. Just remember, this is my home turf and here *I* make the rules. You won't be able to make a move without my knowing about it. Every breath you take, every word you speak. Mine.'

'So I'm to be kept a prisoner, is that it?' She lifted her head proudly, so that he would see she was not intimidated.

'If it's a prison it's one of your own making,' he said with a grim satisfaction that silenced her completely.

His home was a complete surprise. Along a street of Paddington's distinctive terraced houses, some crumbling, some restored to a new lease of life, they turned into the gates of a high brick wall. Unnervingly, it reminded Jessica of another high wall and she swallowed as the wrought iron responded to an electronic signal and clanged shut behind the car. They were in a brick courtyard outside a long, squat, rectangular building. It, too, was built of brick, the surface of which was pitted with decades of Sydney pollution.

'It looks like an old warehouse,' she said nervously, wondering if he was going to shut her up in some dusty, forgotten storage house until she was required.

'It was.'

He opened the red door in the windowless wall and Jessica gasped as she stepped inside. The contrast between exterior and interior was breathtaking. Instead of a dimly lit cavern there was a light, bright series of interlocking puzzles. Daylight flooded in great banks of shuttered skylights that ran along the roof. There was no ceiling as such, just a crisscrossing of steel beams, painted black, with adjacent piping and air-conditioning conduits painted a glossy red.

The brick walls were whitewashed and the carpet that stretched through the massive living area was also white. The sparse arrangement of furniture had an almost Oriental simplicity that was echoed in the rice-paper shades which hung in clusters from the steel beams and everywhere black and red accentuated the purity of the white background.

Slowly Jessica followed Matthew's lead, forgetting her antagonism in her fascination. Focal point of the living area was the huge saucer-like black bowl that formed a central fireplace and the sleek black visor that swept down from the roof to hover above it.

The interior seemed to have been created on a series of single-step levels, the spaces divided by an endless array of sliding doors and panels that created new perceptions as they were opened and closed. She wondered at the kind of man who could own two such different homes—that cluttered period piece in England, and this modern, minimilist's paradise.

As they moved further back in the building, along a narrow panelled corridor, Jessica was aware of a new quality of quiet. Here the doors and walls were insulated to absorb the sounds of the rest of the house. Through half-open doors she glimpsed intriguing splashes of light and colour. The skylights overhead were narrower and the rooms to each side appeared to have conventional windows.

'This is your room.' He slid open a door and motioned her through in front of him.

White, with accents of brown and gold. The bed was sunk into a carpeted platform, the sheets and pillows dark brown, the duvet patterned with bamboo

the gold tones of which found a match in the pliable
vertical blinds which gently billowed at the floor-
length window. A glass door let out to a tiny, bricked-
off courtyard, a serene oasis of raked gravel and
stones.

Aware she was being watched, but no longer caring,
Jessica inspected the spacious recessed wardrobe and
cupboards and investigated another door that lead into
an en-suite bathroom. The sunken bath was tiled in
brown and white, like the floor, and there was a
window behind it looking out on to the same
courtyard. There were no blinds and Jessica wondered
if she would ever be able to pluck up the courage to
have a bath.

'It's industrial strength glass, mirrored on the other
side,' came the drawling mockery of her thoughts from
behind her. 'Besides, the whole place is surrounded by
an eight-foot wall.'

'Is that to keep people in or out?' she shot back.

'Stone walls don't make a prison, Jessica. People
do.'

'Will you stop talking about prisons all the time,'
Jessica snapped, brushing rudely past the lean, relaxed
body, 'Where's your room?' A mile away she hoped,
but she knew, almost before he moved, what was
going to happen.

Almost the whole wall opposite her bed slid away to
reveal a mirror version of her room. Her skin prickled
all over to think that their actions too, as they
undressed and performed all the intimate little tasks of
daily living, would also mirror each other.

'Well?' The dark eyes invited her objections, but
she knew him well enough by now to deny him the
pleasure of crushing her futile resistance.

'I hope the door has a lock on it,' she said mildly.

A flicker of disappointment passed over his face.
'None of the interior doors have locks on them. If I

want you, Jessica, I can come and get you wherever you are, whatever you are doing.'

'Really?' she gave him a scornful, flaming smile that had seared many a lesser man. 'You might meet with a nasty shock. One win out of three isn't a particularly good rating.'

'Ah, but then the second bout never really got started, did it? You had outside help on that occasion. Any time you want a rematch...' He trailed off suggestively and they measured glances for a moment. Jessica was tempted to fling down the gauntlet, but common sense prevailed. He would love an excuse to lay hands on her but she wasn't going to be taunted into a fight she might not win.

He came towards her, past her, with that distinctive gliding stride that was part of her own repetoire. In judo, all movements commenced from the hip and with constant practice the smooth, unbroken transfers of balance became second nature in guarding against unexpected attack.

'Come. I'll introduce you.'

To whom? Jessica didn't bother to ask. Hers not to reason why.

The enormous kitchen ran the entire width of the building halfway down its length, between the sleeping and living areas. The floor was black ceramic tile, the fittings stainless steel and chrome, the cupboards lacquered wood. It was an efficient working kitchen, a miracle of gadgetry, and working very efficiently in the centre of it was a black-haired child.

But when Matthew introduced them she saw that it was not a child but a young man, slim to the point of emaciation with dark slanting eyes and ochre skin.

'This is David Ho. He is in charge of the household. Anything that you want, Jessica, ask him. Anything within reason.'

Jessica ignored the arid qualification and shook

hands politely. David didn't look old enough to be in charge of anything, but it was difficult to judge his actual age—he could be anything from fifteen to thirty.

'David is Vietnamese. His wife, Kim, works with him. Is she here?'

'She's out doing the shopping,' David told Matthew, his English almost perfect but with the faintest of American accents. The easy smile he gave his employer told Jessica much about their relationship. So it *was* possible for someone to work in harmony with the swine! 'Mr Farrow called early this morning. He is going to be delayed in Perth a few more days.'

'Good. That'll give Jessica time to become accustomed to things.' *Things*. He meant himself she supposed. 'I won't be here for lunch and I may not be back for dinner. Perhaps you might give Jessica a taste of Vietnamese cooking—she's very fond of Chinese, aren't you, darling?'

Jessica recovered from the casual endearment to send him a fulminating look. 'I love it.' *I hate you.*

He absorbed the silent dagger with a small chuckle.

'Just testing, Jessica. It'll be a dead-giveaway if you look so surprised when I call you pretty names in front of our guests.' He interpreted her sidelong glance at the watchful David Ho. 'I told David and Kim all about you, so don't bother to try any of your wiles on them. Beautiful, but light-fingered, and a compulsive liar. That about sums you up, doesn't it?'

Jessica drew herself up to her full height and gave the two of them an icy look before spinning on her heel and marching out into the lounge, the long straight back an eloquent gesture of contempt for his baiting. She wouldn't lower herself to argue in front of such an obviously partisan audience.

'Don't take it so hard, Jessica.' The hated voice followed her as he collected the briefcase he had left on the huge black leather couch and prepared to depart. 'You've got to accept that your performance needs polishing, and I'm in the ideal position to provide a little constructive criticism. Behave yourself while I'm away.' He paused at the front door to insert his last barb. 'And by the way, I had David take an inventory of the silverware. If there's any missing at the end of your stay I shall know where to look.'

If Jessica had had the strength she would have thrown the couch at the back of his arrogant head.

Angrily she prowled about the house, defiantly exploring every room, trying to find a jarring note. She found none. It was all quite exquisite, a modern adaption of Japanese decor. The technological wizardry of the modern age—stereo, television and several small computers—were masked behind sliding or folding panels, and even the telephone was a single, delicate piece of white sculpture. Telephones, rather, for there seemed to be one in every room, even in the large, square exercise room she discovered at the rear of the house. There was a familiar cushioned mat resting on the bare, polished wood floor. So this was where the brown belt kept in shape. Rungs climbed the wall and there were various pieces of exercise equipment dotted about, all well-used. There was a sauna and spa pool too, in the outside courtyard.

At her solitary lunch Jessica finally met Kim, who turned out to be even more petite than her husband, with long black hair that flowed like silk down her back. She exchanged a few words with Jessica in heavily accented English and smiled shyly before scuttling away. At least she didn't seem hostile, and she did return to identify each strange dish when Jessica, bewildered by the variety of bowls in front of her, rang the small silver bell on the table.

There was chicken with lemon grass, beef with sesame sauce, small, flat, fried shrimpcakes and deliciously flavoured rice. Jessica, who had an appetite to match her size, ate every morsel. Perhaps there were going to be *some* compensations to her enforced holiday, her first one since her trip to England.

It was not easy to adjust to doing nothing. Jessica was used to having every moment of her day highly organised. Rattling about the house with no one to talk to but Kim and David was enervating rather than restful. She hardly saw Matthew, who was gone by the time she woke in the mornings and frequently not home for dinner, and she actually found herself looking forward to their clashes, just for something to do.

Out of sheer habit she had packed her judogi and found some satisfaction in working her frustrations out in the little gym. Once into the loose, comfortable costume she felt almost at home and there was something reassuring about performing the familiar, ritualistic movements and falls of judo. A sauna afterwards helped steam away her cares. She could almost believe she was incarcerated on a health farm!

The arrival of her baggage had provided a sharp reminder of her position, should she have been in danger of forgetting it. It had arrived the afternoon they did, but Jessica stubbornly refused to give Matthew even the slightest acknowledgment for what turned up was not the one case she had packed, but two! She frowned at the second case which certainly looked familiar, and checked the label. It bore her name and destination.

Slowly she flicked open the clasp and raised the lid. Her mouth set when she saw the contents . . . all the glittery, glamoury dresses she had deliberately omitted to pack.

'Damn!' She collapsed on to the side of her bed, hurling silent curses at her tormentor. Foiled again.

Obviously he had gone behind her back and sweet-talked Jill into packing these for her. She wondered what fresh lies he had told. Something embarrassing. Hearts and flowers, probably, he was good at that! Well, he couldn't *force* her to wear them. Defiantly she closed the case with a snap and over the next few days stuck to her skirts and blouses. What a swine the man was!

One evening Matthew was home for dinner. He joined her in the lounge in time for a drink, showered and shaved, wearing a black fitted shirt and black corduroy trousers. Both looked well-cut and expensive and hugged the muscular contours of his body with unnecessary zeal. Jessica was annoyed that she should notice the way the rib of the corduroy curved around his slim hips and long, powerful thighs. So he had a good body... there was no need to flaunt it at *her*. The shirt, half open, revealed the gleam of his chest under a smattering of red-brown curls. At least he wasn't wearing a gold chain and bracelet, she thought snidely as he handed her a miniscule sherry and took the couch opposite her chair with a generous vodka and tonic. A lock of dark, wavy hair fell over one dark brow and he casually ran it back with a square-clipped hand. He could do with a haircut, thought Jessica critically, it grew thickly with a vitality to match the rest of him. Her own hair was loose, the dress one he had seen before. Let him know she wasn't seeking his approval in any way.

'What do you think of my house, now you've lived in it for a few days?' he asked, after a few minutes silence.

'It's beautiful,' Jessica allowed with grudging truth. 'I can't understand——' she stopped, aware of dangerous ground.

'The house in Devon wasn't of my choosing,' he supplied evenly, aware of the trend of her thoughts.

'Here I allowed myself entirely selfish freedom. I have no time for extraneous detail.'

'You have no time for anything,' Jessica murmured darkly.

One dark eyebrow rose mockingly. 'Feeling neglected, Jessica? Don't you enjoy being a kept woman?'

'Kept is exactly right!' she said, annoyed. 'It's like being in purdah. David won't let me out of the house.' He had been polite, pleasant even, but adamant. 'I hate being shut up, sitting around all day bored out of my skull.'

'Really? I would have thought you'd have the intellectual resources to amuse yourself. There are books . . . the television, video, computer. Or are they too taxing? Perhaps you're not so different from Kristin after all.'

'It has nothing to do with intellect,' Jessica glared at him, resenting the slur on her mind, especially when he knew it was untrue. 'I don't want to be amused. I want to be back in New Zealand running my business.'

'No use crying over spilt milk, Jessica. Time enough to run around loose when Kristin gets here. Meanwhile why don't you practice your role . . . start worrying about the colour of your lipstick and what perfume to wear—all the petty concerns that usually fill the life of pampered mistresses.'

Jessica reacted as he knew she would. Her eyes turned the colour of her sherry, amber lights dancing furiously. But he got more than he bargained for.

'My God, how stultifying! Is that what you expect your women to be like . . . no wonder you have problems! Maybe that's what went wrong with your marriage. Did it ever occur to you that your wife might have wanted a career of her own . . . or children to fill her empty life?' She struck at his only known vulnerable point.

'She had a career—in self-fulfilment through self-appreciation,' he said coldly, finishing off his drink, 'and children would have ruined her figure.'

'Did *you* want them?' came out involuntarily, sensing he was speaking the truth.

'I . . . didn't care either way.' This time he wasn't speaking the truth. The lie was in the stiffened angle of his neck and the brooding look he threw around the pristine neatness of the room, as if he was imagining it strewn with toys and alive with the chatter of young voices.

'You would have been mostly an absentee father anyway, since you travelled so much,' she murmured provocatively, and felt a twinge of guilt at the savage look he impaled her with.

'We will not discuss it,' he said through his teeth.

'Oh no, pardon me for forgetting. We mustn't discuss anything meaningful, anything real. Let's just play comfortable charades.'

His mouth quirked suddenly, making the thin lower lip look fuller, more sensual. 'I don't think I could ever feel comfortable with you, Jessica, whatever game we were playing.'

Now what did he mean by that? He seemed genuinely amused, but Matthew was a difficult man to read, he was so changeable.

'It's probably your guilt needling you,' she told him. 'This whole situation is of your own making. But there's still time to change your mind . . .'

'Oh no, Jessica, not until I get my money's worth.' He no longer looked amused. At a quiet word from Kim he lead the way into dinner, silently beginning his soup while Jessica restlessly sought to introduce another bone of contention.

'What did you tell Jill, to con her into packing that case for me?'

'Did it arrive?' He managed a look of surprise as he

took in her smart but familiar dress. 'I thought it might have been misdirected, since you obviously haven't even unpacked it yet.'

'Why should I—there's no one here I need to impress. You did it deliberately, didn't you, out of sheer spite, to embarrass me.'

'I never do anything out of *sheer* spite,' he warned her softly, spoon paused halfway to his mouth. 'I know you inside out, I knew you'd do anything to thwart me even at a risk of humiliating yourself.' He let that sink in. 'Kristin is an extremely beautiful woman, and as fashion conscious as only a rich man's wife can be. She's also very good at making fellow members of her sex feel inferior—a little glamour will help armour you against her.'

Jessica stiffened. 'I can only be made to feel inadequate by people I respect. I hardly think that's going to happen in this case. After all, the stupid woman is infatuated with *you*.'

'Do you have to argue with everything I say?' he said, in a gravelling voice that made him sound unutterably weary. He allowed Kim to take away the bowls and serve a delicious concoction of mixed vegetables while Jessica studied him under her lashes. He did look tired. He had been working twelve- to eighteen-hour days ever since she had been here and was obviously tense over his meeting with Kent Farrow. But his problems were nothing to do with her, she told herself. If he was tired it was his own damned fault . . . he should delegate more.

He took up his fork and then put it down again, looking Jessica directly in the face. 'I think it's time we came to an understanding. We can carry this thing through in one of two ways. The first, and most unpleasant for both of us, is to continue as we are—with you fighting and obstructing me every step of the way, purely on principle of course since the outcome is preordained in my favour. My temper is more than a match for yours and if you want to make our relationship a series of painful and humiliating confrontations so be it—like you I never back away from a fight.

'On the other hand, the next few weeks could be relatively painless if you would accept the realities of your situation and make the best of them. Behave as a guest and be treated as one.'

'Why should I make things easy for you? It seems to me that all the advantages lie on your side.'

'A truce works both ways.' Satisfied he had her interest, albeit wary, he began to eat. 'You'll get a chance to recoup your strength, study your opposition in peace. You must realise by now that your approach is all wrong, that you're not getting anywhere by direct attack, you don't know me well enough. Remember the judo principle? Give way to strength, let your opponent defeat himself with your assistance.'

'You're *inviting* me to defeat you?'

His smile made her blood boil. 'Let's just say I'm not afraid of the attempt . . . *after* the agreement is signed. You know what I want you to do. If you tackle it with the same determination to succeed with which you tackle everything else in your life I see no reason why I should have to mention it again. Let's co-exist for the duration. I can concentrate on my work, and you can relax and enjoy your all-expenses-paid holiday.'

He would still be getting the better part of the deal, but Jessica was unbearably tempted. She still felt bruised and battered by circumstances and needed time to think, to plan.

'Truce, Jessica?' He extended his hand across the table, lean and strong.

'Truce . . . Matthew.' She put her hand into his, felt the hardness of bone and sinew and in turn let him feel her considerable strength. The struggle was silent and it told Jessica what all her instincts had sensed— that his words were only a thinly disguised device to gain her co-operation, that the war had now gone underground.

That night she tossed and turned, trying to figure the angles. So far Matthew had only brought her to her knees, and she had fought him every inch of the way, giving him only the barest minimum of satisfaction. He wanted, had always wanted, to have her completely defenceless, only he didn't have the time or energy to devote to her right now. He wanted submission, mental as well as physical. In fact, of the two, she felt that psychological domination of her was the more important to him.

She shivered in the warm bed, burrowing down to blot out the sound of quiet breathing that emanated from the dark room across the open space. It seemed loud in the blackness, surrounding her, preventing her from escaping him even in sleep. She wouldn't let him gain complete ascendency over her, she couldn't; she doubted she was capable of allowing it without destroying herself.

More importantly she felt, deep within her, on an instinctive level, that to give Matthew total victory would be as dangerous for him as it was for her. He was already contemptuous and distrustful of women. By resisting him Jessica was forcing him to respect her. To a certain extent it was his respect for her as an opponent that had forced the truce. If she continued to resist, he would have to admit that there were women in the world worthy of respect, as self-confident and self-reliant as men, different yet no less intelligent, courageous, strong.

She would prove that to him, if it was the last thing she did!

CHAPTER SEVEN

THE few days of strength-conserving quiet were sorely needed and Jessica was even more grateful for them when she finally met the Farrows. She had thought there might be some empathy between her and Kristin Farrow—both, so to speak, victims of Matthew Grieve. But Kristin was all Matthew had accused her of being . . . and more!

Kristin was indeed beautiful; small and dark and sultry. She was a few years older than Jessica but skilfully concealed it beneath a captivating feminine helplessness that grated on Jessica's tender nerves. The woman was about as helpless as a black widow spider, and the first time she opened her mouth, it was to spread sugary venom.

'Goodness, Jessica,' she gasped as they were introduced. 'Aren't you tall—and you're not even wearing heels!'

Jessica agreed pleasantly. 'Some people find it intimidating; then again, some people *like* being intimidated.' She slid a smouldering glance at the bland-faced man beside her. In a few words she had set the scene . . . Matthew was firmly enmeshed in her toils, and enjoying it.

Jessica shook hands with Kent Farrow, seeing in his faded but sharply restless grey eyes the reasons for Matthew's concern. Kent was shorter than Jessica by at least six inches and of a sturdy build that indicated he could easily run to fat. He was in his late fifties but his craggy face showed no signs of slackness. That and the careful cut of his modern suit told Jessica that here was a man very conscious of the passing of time. He

97

was here to divest himself of some of his power, to begin a slow process of retirement. He would always be rich, but he would never wield more power than he did at this moment, and he knew it. He would resent Matthew's youth and stamina even as he relied on it and perhaps, just perhaps, he was looking for a way to back out of this deal without loss of face, an excuse to retain the reins of command a little longer.

'Matt has told me all about you.' He shook Jessica's hand vigorously, speaking with a broad Australian twang. 'I'm glad you're here to keep Kristin company. She gets bored on these business trips when I'm tied up all day, don't you, sweetheart?'

'Oh I'm sure Jessica and I will find lots in common,' his wife murmured slyly, dark blue eyes flickering towards Matthew.

Conversation with Kristin was hard-going, Jessica discovered over the next three days. Away from attentive males she lost all her scintillating sweetness, and became a tireless interrogator.

'Are you a model?' she asked Jessica, almost as soon as they were alone. 'You're certainly tall enough.'

Jessica supposed she should be flattered. 'No. I have ... er ... investments.'

'Matthew being one of them, I suppose.' With a coy, inviting smile that repelled Jessica.

'Mmmm, no, he's more of a takeover,' she replied calmly and was pleased to note the other woman's frustration. Deliberately she adopted a rather abstracted air that enabled her to evade the most blatant probes, though sometimes desperation led her to make sarcastic comments that completely confounded Kristin. It wasn't that she was a particularly stupid woman, but she was vain and her vanity made her narrow-minded. She had no ambition, save that of spending her husband's money, no appreciation of life outside her wealthy cocoon. On the other hand she

GIVE YOUR HEART TO HARLEQUIN®

FREE!

Mail this heart today!

AND WE'LL GIVE YOU
4 FREE BOOKS, A
FREE PEN AND WATCH SET,
AND A FREE MYSTERY GIFT!

SEE INSIDE!

☙ IT'S A ☙
HARLEQUIN HONEYMOON
A SWEETHEART
OF A FREE OFFER!

4 NEW "HARLEQUIN PRESENTS"—FREE! Take a "Harlequin Honeymoon" with four exciting romances—yours FREE from Harlequin Reader Service! Each of these hot-off-the-presses novels brings you all the passion and tenderness of today's greatest love stories...your free passports to bright new worlds of love and foreign adventure!

But wait...there's <u>even more</u> to this great <u>free offer</u>...

HARLEQUIN PEN AND WATCH SET—ABSOLUTELY FREE! You'll love your personal Harlequin Pen and Watch Set. Perfect for daytime...elegant enough for evening. The watch has a genuine leather strap and replaceable battery. The watch and the stylish matching pen are yours free with this offer!

SPECIAL EXTRAS—FREE! You'll get our free monthly newsletter, packed with news on your favorite writers, upcoming books, and more. Four times a year, you'll receive our members' magazine, Harlequin Romance Digest! <u>Best of all,</u> you'll periodically <u>receive our special-edition "Harlequin Bestsellers," yours to preview for ten days without charge!</u>

MONEY-SAVING HOME DELIVERY! Join Harlequin Reader Service and enjoy the <u>convenience</u> of previewing eight new books every month, delivered right to your home. Each book is yours for only $1.75—<u>20¢ less per book</u> than what you pay in stores! Great savings plus total convenience add up to a sweetheart of a deal for <u>you!</u>

FU 8/85

START YOUR HARLEQUIN HONEYMOON TODAY—
JUST COMPLETE, DETACH & MAIL YOUR FREE OFFER CARD!

HARLEQUIN READER SERVICE

⌒§ FREE OFFER CARD ≥⌒

FREE PEN AND WATCH SET

FREE HOME DELIVERY

PLUS AN EXTRA BONUS "MYSTERY GIFT"!

4 FREE BOOKS

PLACE HEART STICKER HERE

☐ YES! Please send me my four HARLEQUIN PRESENTS® books, free, along with my free Pen and Watch Set and Mystery Gift! Then send me eight new HARLEQUIN PRESENTS books every month, as they come off the presses, and bill me at just $1.75 per book (20¢ less than retail), with no extra charges for shipping and handling. If I am not completely satisfied, I may return a shipment and cancel at any time. The free books, Pen, Watch and Mystery Gift remain mine to keep!

108 CIP CAKD

FIRST NAME_____ LAST NAME_____
                          (PLEASE PRINT)

ADDRESS_____ APT._____

CITY_____

PROV./STATE_____ POSTAL CODE/ZIP_____

PRINTED IN U.S.A.

BUSINESS REPLY CARD

First Class   Permit No. 717   Buffalo, NY

Postage will be paid by addressee

NO POSTAGE
NECESSARY
IF MAILED
IN THE
UNITED STATES

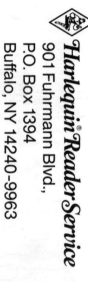

Harlequin Reader Service®

901 Fuhrmann Blvd.,
P.O. Box 1394
Buffalo, NY 14240-9963

was obviously just the kind of wife that Kent required—beautiful, poised, sophisticated and self-centred enough to know which side her bread was buttered. She was a bolster to his ego, proof to the world that he was capable of winning, and keeping, possession of beautiful women. That he also loved her was obvious from the way he kept watch on her, especially when she was with Matthew.

Jessica didn't blame him. Matthew was being infuriatingly passive. He might be wary of offending Kristin, but surely he was carrying inoffensiveness too far! He smilingly allowed Kristin to flutter around him like a jewelled butterfly, to tease and entertain him. It was left up to Jessica to play the heavy, and draw all Kristin's veiled fire. Matthew was giving a wonderful performance of a man overwhelmed by a cunning, determined woman. 'Of course I find you attractive,' he seemed to be silently admitting to Kristin, 'but what can I do . . . Jessica has me tied up in knots.'

As the villain of the piece Jessica had to put up with not only Kristin's barbs, but also Matthew's play-kisses and play-caresses. It was all she could do to restrain herself from slapping his head off.

Once his guests had settled in, Matthew bore Kent off to begin negotiations in earnest and most days they spent closeted with their lawyers and advisers at his office in the city. But Kent insisted on taking time off to squire Kirstin to this function or that. Jessica could sense that Matthew was impatient with the constant interruptions but reluctant to force the pace. He was definitely preoccupied and as a result their precarious truce continued to survive, largely because they were hardly ever in conversation alone together and when they were Matthew's responses were so mechanical Jessica doubted he even knew what they were.

One afternoon they all met for lunch at one of the city's most famous Chinese restaurants. It was situated at The Rocks, the site of the first European settlement in Australia and now an exclusive shopping district and tourist attraction. From the second floor of a restored Colonial warehouse, the restaurant had a panoramic view of Sydney Harbour. The famous harbour bridge arched almost directly overhead and to their right the Opera House raised the majestic sails of its roof above the sparkling waters which surrounded it on three sides.

Jessica, feet aching from yet another of Kristin's interminable shopping binges, indulged herself shamelessly as she discovered that the food was as spectacular as the view. Having learned something about Vietnamese cookery from David and Kim she could appreciate the subtle differences in the classic Chinese dishes before her. With a hearty appetite she worked her way through the seafood rolls served on nutty, deep-fried lettuce; the big, plump mussels served juicily in their shells smothered in a rich and fiery chilli sauce; the lobster and beef which preceded the glorious event of Peking Duck.

'I must say I envy your appetite,' said Kristin wonderingly as she watched Jessica roll up yet another piece of dark-red, crispy duck skin and white flesh garnished with cucumber and spring onion, into a pale, speckled pancake. 'I couldn't eat half the amount you do.'

'She's a big girl, she has to keep her strength up,' Matthew grinned, leaning over to catch a drip of plum sauce as it oozed from the pancake on to Jessica's chin. As she often did when he touched her she stiffened as his warm fingertip brushed the sensitive corner of her mouth and his eyes darkened with annoyance. Jessica made herself relax as she glanced over at Kristin and saw that she had watched the small byplay intently.

'I'm lucky to be a perfect size ten,' she said, picking daintily at her food. 'I have no trouble finding clothes to fit me, but we have a terrible time with you, don't we, Jessie.'

Jessica clenched her teeth at the ghastly contraction of her name. She was proud of her size fourteen, considering her height and build. She suspected that Kristin deliberately sought out boutiques that specialised in frills and flounces and yards of gathered taffetas that made Jessica look like a wrestler in drag every time she was sweetly browbeaten into trying something on.

'In fact,' Kristin chewed thoughtfully, 'you've hardly bought a single thing at all. It's almost as if you don't *want* to spend any money. Doesn't Matthew give you enough?'

Jessica longed to fling out that she didn't want him to give her anything, even the credit cards he had thrust upon her. She would never leech on a man in the way that Kristin did.

'I can never give her enough,' Matthew pressed his thigh threateningly against Jessica's under cover of the table. 'She's insatiable, aren't you, darling?'

Jessica jerked her leg away from the heat of his and flushed at the suggestive mockery.

'You can still make her blush!' Kent laughed his appreciation. 'Oh, Matt, you have a rare gem there.'

'How long have you two been together?' Kristin asked smoothly, probably never having blushed in her life.

'Not long enough.' Matthew smiled blandly and Jessica willed Kristin to drop the subject, but she was like a dog with a half-buried bone.

'You met in England I think you said. Were you still married, then, Matt?'

There was an imperceptible rise in tension between the two men at the table. Kristin was sweetly implying that matrimony was no barrier to Matthew's interest.

'Lisa and I were separated for some time before the

divorce,' Matthew supplied coolly after a brief hesitation that felt like years. 'But as it happens, Jessica and I didn't even properly introduce ourselves until we met again in Auckland. Before that we'd only spoken a few words to each other . . . though I never forgot her.'

'And what was it you found so unforgettable?' Kristin probed with a touch of acid.

Jessica caught the glitter in Matthew's eyes. Damn Kristin for reminding him. She braced herself for something outrageous and she wasn't disappointed.

'Her strength, I think. The first time I saw her she knocked me out. The second time I was really bitten. The third time *I* did the biting.'

'Sounds more like a fight than a love affair,' said Kristin suspiciously while Jessica tried to conquer an urge to giggle at Matthew's exact presentation of the facts.

'We have our moments, don't we darling?' He gave Jessica a melting look. 'You trying to put a ring through my nose and me trying to put one through yours.'

'All this talk about rings,' Kristin pounced coyly, hoping to cause optimum embarrassment. 'Does that mean what I think it means . . .?'

Kent looked expectantly at Matthew while Jessica rushed into speech. She was not about to be dragged any deeper into deception.

'Well, Matt *has* been putting the pressure on,' she enjoyed the trapped expression that flitted across his face, 'but I don't really want to settle down yet.'

'Oh, really?' Kristin smiled, kitten-like. 'You prefer variety to fidelity. How modern of you. I suppose you look down on those of us who put home and family ahead of everything else, as being too old-fashioned.'

'Not at all,' said Jessica holding on to her temper as she sensed the male censure at the table. 'I just want to make certain that when I do settle down it's with the right person. I don't want to end up a bored and restless wife, always regretting that I grabbed for security at the expense of self-respect.' In case that was too pointed she shot a dazzling look at a tense Matt. 'Besides, Matt thrives on challenge, don't you, *darling*? You wouldn't be so eager for my company if you could dominate me too easily.'

Her smile slipped when he took her up on it, bringing her hand up from her lap and crushing it into a fist as he brought it to his lips. 'Mmm, I must admit that I enjoy our skirmishing. Losing to you has its . . . er . . . pleasurable consolations.' He wouldn't allow her to pull her hand away, holding it as he held her gaze, with a compelling strength that made her tingle with excitement.

'I didn't realise you went in for muscular women, Matt,' Kristin shuddered delicately. 'I thought that you liked them small and dainty.' Like Lisa, Jessica guessed . . . and like Kristin.

'Tastes change, Kristin,' said Matt, dropping Jessica's hand. 'It also depends on which muscles they use, and how.'

Jessica gave him a fulminating look and a sharp kick under the table when he winked wickedly. He didn't even wince, but caught her ankle between his shins and held it there, slipping a hand down to stroke her immobile knee every now and then. Unable to struggle Jessica sat, flushing, aware that the two across the table noticed Matt's straying hand.

She ought to have been humiliated, but she was too busy trying to cope with the fiery heat that streaked up her thigh to nestle in her stomach. Every nerve in her body seemed attuned to that soft, intermittent caress. Kristin's barely concealed chagrin only added to her strange elation. She knew that Matthew intended this public affirmation of his desire as a private form of punishment. So why didn't she feel punished? Why was she enjoying this? The threat of a logical answer sent her thoughts into retreat, and the next time Matt stroked her she dug her nails into the back of his hand.

That evening, when Matthew strode into her room, his face dark and moody, she braced herself for a confrontation.

'What do you want?' she demanded, having given up questioning his right to march in on her whenever he chose. Fortunately she already had her long, old-gold gown zipped up and was donning a single tear-drop pearl in front of the mirror.

'What do you think, after your behaviour this afternoon!' He swept the inky black of his dinner jacket behind his hips to reveal a dazzling white shirt front in stark contrast.

'I thought I behaved rather well, considering.' Jessica took up her brush and used it vigorously on her flowing locks.

'Oh yes, you're great at the bitchery but you haven't got the substance to back it up,' he ground out, irritated by her coolness. 'You're *supposed* to be my mistress, yet you blush like a virgin every time there's mention of sex, and you stiffen up every time I lay a hand on you. Do you think Farrow won't notice? Don't be taken in by that rough-diamond friendliness, he's got a mind like a steel trap.'

'And his wife has a mouth like one!' Jessica threw down the brush and whirled around.

'What are you worrying about, you give as good as you get—though you could ask her for a few lessons on how to please a man.'

'Oh, really? She doesn't seem to be pleasing you very much—that's why I'm here, remember? I'm damned if I'm going to maul you about like she does, and hang on your every word as if you're a god. Real

women don't act like that ... at least, not with real
men.'

'You bitch——'

'Takes one to know one, darling,' drawled Jessica
standing tall, her head flung back in challenge.

'Well, whatever I am, I'm not frigid,' he snarled
back at her, a lock of his carefully groomed hair falling
forward as he, too, lifted his head. Jessica wished she
had put on higher heels so that she could spit fire at
him from his own level. 'I don't cringe at normal
human contact.'

'No, I realise that. It puffs up your ego, doesn't it,
to have that stupid woman draping herself all over
you. Maybe *I* am more discriminating. Maybe I like to
keep sex where it belongs—in the bedroom.'

His eyebrows shot up. 'In the bedroom?' He
laughed in a way that made Jessica want to hit him.
'What an extremely boring sex life you must lead,
Jessica.'

'If you wanted a trollop you should have hired a girl
off the streets. You wouldn't know class if it hit you in
the face. It may be Kristin's style to be all over a man like
a rash but that's not the way *I* act when I'm in love.'

'How the hell would you know, you've never been
in love, unless you count that over-heated, over-aged
Romeo when you were seventeen.'

Jessica gasped and flushed. God, his detective must
have dug deep, she'd almost forgotten about that
painful first crush. Paul had only wanted one thing
from her, and when she had baulked at the last minute
anger had peeled away his charm, and his contempt
for her naïvity had been devastating. With the
experience of his over thirty years he had quickly
reduced her to tears, shattering her romantic illusions.
She had never cried over a man since.

'Even when I was seventeen I didn't moon,' she lied
stiffly. 'And I have no intention of starting now.'

'And *I* have no intention of letting this deal slide out from under me because of your squeamishness. Kent is acting very cagily. I'm having a hard time pinning him down to specifics. You must have seen the way he looks at Kristin, he's uptight . . . he's backing off any commitment.'

'Might you be misjudging her influence? Maybe he's being cagey for an entirely different reason,' said Jessica tentatively, realising that Matthew's anger was a symptom of frustration rather than a result of her behaviour.

'There *is* nothing else, not according to my information, and the source is usually accurate. You've seen Kristin in action, she specialises in creating trouble . . . it's a damned vocation!' He ran a tired hand through the sleekness of his hair, his harassment a tacit plea for understanding, to which Jessica responded.

'I'm doing my best, but she's a hard woman to discourage. Have you ever considered plastic surgery?'

She had hoped to lighten his mood and for a moment she succeeded. Humour washed away his angry fatigue. 'My face or my wallet? I was hoping I wouldn't have to do anything quite that drastic.'

'What you have done is quite drastic enough.'

'I'm quite aware of that!' came out in a kind of groan that had them staring at each other in surprise. He half shook his head. 'Look, just do what I brought you here to do, OK?' It was like a slap in the face after that tiny moment of contact and he swore at her expression and began violently: 'If you don't . . .'

Jessica waited for the by-now familiar threat, but instead he trailed off with another muffled curse, spun on his heel and left. Was conscience finally catching up with the king? Jessica hesitated to read any significance into Matthew's sudden reluctance to apply force where he thought it was required but she couldn't help the tiny leap of hope.

That evening she played hostess with a new warmth and wit, drawing the attention of both males in spite of Kristin's persistent attempts to shut her out of the conversation.

Thwarted at the dinner table, Kristin insisted on dancing after dinner. The lights were low, the music soft, and Jessica was not amused at the way Matt allowed Kristin to nestle up to him. She felt a surge of possessive rage. Whose tormentor was he supposed to be? He was *hers*.

'May I cut in?' A neat little manoeuvre left Kristin back with her husband.

'I thought for a moment there that you were going to throw her over your shoulder,' Matthew murmured in her ear as he linked his arms around her waist.

'I didn't think I could manage both of you, you were practically glued together,' she replied with soft acidity.

A laugh vibrated against her breasts. 'You're so beautiful when you're jealous.' His hands slid to her hips, one thigh moving between hers as he turned her, and Jessica trembled at the hard shift of his body against her softness. She tried to ease away but he stopped her, pulling her even closer.

'Now, now, Jessica, this was your idea remember.' His brandy-warm breath slid across her cheek and lightly caressed her mouth. Jessica couldn't stop her trembling, imagining his mouth replacing his breath.

He chuckled again. 'You're learning, Amazon, you're learning. Those little tremors are very effective . . . as if you can't wait to get into bed with me. Have you ever made love standing up?'

Jessica turned her hot face into the fine thread of his jacket. Effective, and very unwelcome. She didn't want to be aware of the muscles in his thighs, the nudge of his hips, the power in his chest and arms. They made her feel soft, vulnerable ... all the things it was vital she *not* feel. Determinedly she tried to distance herself from her body. She succeeded at the cost of a night's sleep, for once the necessity of maintaining her composure passed she was hit by a nervous reaction that denied her the ability to relax. Not even her breathing exercises helped. For once, judo let her down. What on earth was happening to her? Was she coming to pieces?

In the morning it was back into battle again. Another shopping trip, this time to jewellery stores. Jessica used her credit cards with a vengeance, hoping to shock Matthew with her extravagance. Let him sweat a little, though she intended to leave every single purchase behind her when she left.

'You don't know very much about Matt, do you, Jessie?' Kristin declared, when they repaired to a bistro for lunch, and she ordered her usual salad.

'How much can we ever know about another human being?' Jessica shrugged, through a mouthful of garlic bread.

'But you don't know *anything*,' Kristin persisted.

Except for what I've gleaned from you and your husband, thought Jessica, a wry smile touching her lips. In her efforts to pry information out of Jessica, Kristin had proved to be a mine of it herself. Jessica had learned that Matthew was not the self-made man she had thought him to be. His father had been a highly successful property speculator and had left a fortune to his son when he and his wife were killed in a car accident. With no other relations, fourteen-year-old Matt spent the rest of his teenage years at school and university, in the guardianship of a trust board. He had inherited full control at twenty-five and, within a few years of his inheritance, had doubled his assets and branched out into the lucrative field of electronics.

'The important thing is what we feel about each other, not what we know,' said Jessica, striving for casualness.

'We all know what *you* feel,' said Kristin bitchily. 'You may spout on about not wanting to settle down but if Matt asked you you'd marry him like a shot. You think that if you hang around long enough he'll fall into your lap.'

'Actually that's not what I think at all,' said Jessica, hating the other woman's constant barbs.

'You don't have to pretend with me, Jessie, Matt's not around to hear you now.'

'Could we change the subject, please?' The high-pitched, girlish voice was as subtle as a pneumatic drill, and just as painful.

'You know, you've misjudged Matt if you think that he goes for all that women's rights stuff—' it had been a topic of dinner conversation more than once '—when it comes right down to it he's like any other man, he'll choose a wife who fits in with his life, not one who tries to compete with him all the time. Men use women like you when it suits them, but when it comes to the crunch they all like to be boss in their own home. You might remember that next time you start foisting your feminist opinions on everyone.'

'I do not foist my opinions on people.' Jessica felt her ire rising, rapidly outstripping her self-control.

'Listen to yourself sometime, Jessie,' Kristin advised smoothly. 'It really can be quite boring. Matt got enough of that kind of rubbish at university. God, I remember how we used to laugh about some of the pompous girls who tried to impress him with their dreary brains.'

Alarm bells sounded deafeningly. Jessica put down the fork she had been using to poke at her prawns. 'You knew Matt when he was at university?'

Kristin's eyes widened in the tiny silence. 'Do you

mean you didn't know? Didn't he tell you? Goodness!'
She sounded unsure whether Jessica was joking, then,
when she saw that she wasn't her eyes lit with malicious
triumph. 'We practically lived together, oh, for ages!'

Why in the *hell* hadn't he mentioned it? Jessica felt a
helpless, storming rage. *Why?*

'I guess we both feel that the past shouldn't
interfere with the present.' She struggled to sound
convincing.

'Or maybe he just doesn't want to let you into his
life,' Kristin said smugly. 'Matt doesn't just trust
anyone. And where there's no trust, there's not much
of a relationship is there? Matt used to talk to me
about *everything*. He was mad about me ... I was the
one who left Matt, not the other way around. That's
what's making poor Kent so nervy ... he thinks I
might want to turn the clock back.'

'Your husband knows?' exclaimed Jessica hollowly,
the food she had swallowed rising up into her throat.

'Of course, it's not a secret.. That's why I'm so
surprised that Matt didn't tell you. Maybe it was too
painful for him. He pleaded with me not to go, but I
was young and silly in those days ... I didn't know a
good thing when I saw it. Now I do ... that's why
we've come on this little trip. I told Kent that he
should be spending more time at home with me,
instead of working himself into the ground. Matt was
the obvious choice for a deal. As for the other well ...
it'll be almost like keeping it all in the family, won't
it?' She smiled, showing sharp, even, teeth white
against her careful tan. 'Goodness, if everyone went
through life trying to avoid their ex-lovers there'd be
no business conducted at *all*. Kent trusts me. At least
there's more honesty between *us* than there is between
you and Matt.'

That evening the Farrows dined out with friends as
Jessica paced the floor, waiting for Matthew to arrive

home. It was after eleven when he finally appeared and he hardly had time to drop his briefcase before she hurled her accusations at his head.

'Why didn't you tell me that she was your mistress?'

He took off his jacket wearily and turned to survey her as she faced him aggressively, her hair tumbling loose around her angry face, her breasts rising and falling under her cinnamon dress.

'I wondered when she'd get around to it. I suppose she's been hinting that I'm secretly pining for the old days. Forget it, Jessica, it just shows how desperate she's getting.'

'Forget it!' Jessica spluttered. 'You lied to me! You told me——'

'What does it matter now?' he cut in impatiently, loosening his tie and unbuttoning his white collar. 'My relationship with Kristin is long dead and she knows it. I've acquired a lot more discrimination with regard to women since her time. It makes no difference to your position, so I saw no point in adding to the complications by telling you.'

'No point! She's even more suspicious now! And so am I——'

'Control yourself, Jessica,' he said coldly, across her outraged yell. 'I'm really not in the mood for this right now.'

'And *he* knows too. I think its disgusting. No wonder you were worried about the deal going sour. Is he out to get you, is that the problem? Were they married when you had your "relationship"? Were *you*?'

He moved a step closer, his eyes darkening. 'Neither of us were. I don't make love to other men's wives,' he said rigidly.

'Huh!' Jessica tossed her head on a snort.

'I happen to believe in marital fidelity,' he bit at her and this time Jessica laughed her scorn.

He grabbed her and gave her a violent shake. 'Oh yes, you might find that funny you thieving, lying, bitch, but it happens to be the truth. I was never unfaithful to Lisa, *never*. I knew she was restless but I trusted her. I was too damned busy to do anything else, too blind sweating my guts out to keep her on easy street.'

Jessica was transfixed by his dark, tormented expression.

'Did you love her?' she whispered, trying to ease out of his painful grip, appalled that, after all, she might have had a hand in smashing something far more delicate and precious than his pride that night in Devon.

'Love her?' There was a bleak self-contempt in his voice. 'What was there to love? I was never a husband at all, I was a mirror for her own desires. She was beautiful, well-bred, well-connected ... sweet as honey until she got my ring on her finger. If I thought I was in love I was pretty soon disillusioned. Money and sex, that's what made her world go around. Only while she was urging me to go out and provide the one she sought elsewhere for the other.'

'Then why on earth did you stay married for so long, if that's how things were?'

Matthew dropped her arm like a hot coal and moved away. 'Because I hate failure!' A cynical expression crossed his face and he turned, full of self-mockery. 'Besides ... as long as she was beautiful, poised and discreet she served a purpose. Everyone thought we were a "lovely couple". She even deigned to share her bed with me when I needed "relief". What could be more convenient?'

'Convenience is a cold companion,' Jessica murmured, seeing the heart of truth in that first, blurted statement. The rest was window dressing, the pride's defence.

A sour smile. 'I had my work, a business to run . . . that absorbed most of my energy. Ironically that's when I made most of my money.'

'So why does that one failure make you so bitter? Lots of people have unsuccessful marriages, it's not a crime. Why measure yourself against a single failure when you have so much success to call your own?'

His eyes drifted around the quietly elegant room, as if the answer lay there. 'Business is different. It comes easy, it always has. Maybe that was the problem. Maybe I expected everything else to fall just as easily into place. Christ, at university I almost fell for Kristin . . . she was so full of social effervescence, so different from me—I was inclined to over-seriousness . . . hardly the action of a man destined to succeed in personal relationships!'

'She said you were mad about her,' revealed Jessica without compunction, not doubting who the liar was.

His gesture of distate was explicit. 'Thank God I wasn't that stupid, she was fun to have around but even then she was a bit of a trouble-maker. A pity the experience didn't seem to teach me anything. If you think Kristin is a bitch you should meet Lisa.'

'Do you hate her, Lisa, I mean?'

'I hate what she *did*, I hate what I allowed her to do.'

'What do you mean?' asked Jessica softly, feeling that she was on the edge of understanding a great mystery, of discovering the real Matthew Grieve.

'I suppose you're enjoying this,' he accused, his voice thick with the tormented desire to spew out the poison his body had stored for so long.

Jessica shook her head, willing him not to stop now. 'I'm only trying to understand.'

Her passive attitude and quiet eyes succeeded where feminine curiosity couldn't. 'I'm sure you'll find it amusing. I was blind, you see. I thought that if I didn't care, it wouldn't matter ... But it did. Because it cut part of me off from myself. I was only functioning on a single level, a public level, privately ...' he swallowed, and forced himself on, avoiding Jessica's eyes. '... In the end, when it was too late, I realised how I had pandered to her greed. She thought she could do what she liked with impunity, that she was safe ... I would never leave her for another woman. She proved her power over me quite graphically.'

He looked at her then, and her blank stare seemed to fill him with a raw anger. 'God, do I have to spell it out for you? She castrated me. In the end even she, with all her skill, couldn't arouse me. Nothing could. No one, though God knows I went frantic trying. *And she laughed.*'

Jessica couldn't take it in. Was he actually claiming ...? Ridiculous! Matt was so virile, so confident, so *male*. He wore his sex-appeal like a second skin ... it was one of the first things that she had noticed about him. Matt impotent?

'I don't believe it!' The words were jerked out of her involuntarily. 'You're lying. Why are you lying?'

On the verge of throttling her for daring to call him a liar about something he had found devastatingly painful, Matthew found himself looking down at her stunned face. She looked flushed, bewildered, and utterly disbelieving. She looked as if she was prepared to fight him over the lie. The knowledge had the force of a blow. He felt the powerful surge in his loins, the sudden intoxicating rush of blood to his head. It tightened his throat, pounded at his temples, his wrists, his groin. At this moment if he took a step, he knew it would be a macho swagger. She might hate him, despise him, hold him in complete contempt ... but she had never, never, doubted his masculinity. And never would.

He couldn't stop the smile which spread and spread across his face. 'It's the truth.' He had never dreamed it would be so easy to admit. As he watched the horrified realisation creep into Jessica's warm brown eyes he was amazed to feel amusement. 'Don't look so aghast,' he drawled in heady pleasure. 'I do assure you that the problem resolved itself once I shook off her vicious little claws.'

'I'm so sorry . . .' whispered Jessica, still trying to take it in.

He lifted a hand to her face, touching its flushed softness. 'Don't be. It wasn't you . . . though maybe I confused you there for a while. You're worlds away from Lisa's kind. And just to show you that's there's no hard feelings . . .' he grinned his wickedly familiar grin '. . . I have a present for you.'

He handed Jessica a plain wrapped package he had placed with his briefcase when he had come in and she took it automatically, trying to fathom where all his bitter anger had gone. One moment he had looked fit to murder her the next he was looking positively smug! Would she *ever* be able to understand the way his mind worked?

CHAPTER EIGHT

GINGERLY, Jessica unwrapped the parcel and blinked stupidly at the contents.

'What on earth——?'

'Think of them as necessary props,' Matthew said as he collapsed on to the couch, his pale yellow shirt a striking contrast to the black leather. He stretched his legs out in front of him, watching as Jessica dropped the open box on to the ceramic coffee table as if it was a nestful of scorpions. 'That Victorian cotton monstrosity you prance around in is a dead giveaway. Kristin's already made some smart remarks about your choice of nightwear. Hardly the kind of thing that a mistress wears to entice her lover.'

'I don't want to entice anyone,' Jessica lied. 'And I'm certainly not going to wear these,' she shoved at a long, sheer black nightgown with a disdainful finger, 'they're indecent.'

'That's the general idea,' he grinned, settling back with a pleasant sense of anticipation as Jessica's eyes began to glitter. 'Anyway, unless you're going to change the habits of a lifetime and sleep in the nude, you've got no choice. I told Kim to get rid of your other night things.'

'You did what!' He wasn't disappointed by her shriek of rage. 'How dare you! You ... you ... ohhh!' And she had wondered why Kim had giggled more than usual this evening. 'I want them back, every one.'

'Too late ... unless you want to feel a heel by ringing the Salvation Army and demanding they return your generous donation.'

'You really are asking for it,' she flung at him and he adopted a lascivious expression.

'I wasn't actually, but I'm game if you are.' A silent glare was her response. 'Oh, come on, Jess ...' how warm and friendly he made the nickname sound. 'What kind of impression do you think it creates? You look sixteen in those other damned things. And virginal white is hardly appropriate.'

'Really? Well, as it so happens, I'm *entitled* to wear white ... which is more than I can say for anyone else in this household,' Jessica shot out furiously.

'Entitled?' His puzzlement made her even angrier ... so he assumed she was promiscuous, did he?

Suddenly the penny dropped and the dark face with its faintly menacing five o'clock shadow lit with an unholy laughter. The black eyes wandered over her tall, statuesque, figure as if seeing her for the first time.

'Jessica? My God, this *is* a night for intimate revelations!' His voice sounded so rich and mellow that she could practically hear the laughter caught in his throat. 'Why?'

Her glare faltered. '*Why!*'

'Yes, why? You can't tell me there haven't been opportunities.' Slyly, he added: 'Share and share alike, now. I told you my secrets.'

'I ... because ... I,' she fumbled, guessing that she did owe him honesty, but finding it hard to encapsulate into words. 'I suppose ... because I can't be casual ... because I've never wanted anyone enough ... because, oh, I don't know—because——' she took a firm grip on herself. 'Look, you happen to believe in fidelity, I happen to believe in chastity.'

'I suppose it's par with that Amazon image of yours,' he said with a gentle, inoffensive humour. 'They remained virgins, too, didn't they, until it was time to kidnap some helpless male and force him to donate his sperm to the greater glory of womankind?'

'They were executed afterwards, too, so I believe,' Jessica hissed at him. She wondered why she wasn't blushing now, why it was that she was enjoying this totally unexpected turn of the conversation.

He threw up his hands. 'Pax. Pax! I really wasn't laughing at you, Jess—at myself I suppose. It never occurred to me that you were an innocent. It's really rather refreshing.'

'I'm sure it is. No doubt you subscribe generously to the double standard,' she said snidely.

'As a matter of fact, I don't. Lisa wasn't a virgin. Nor was Kristin. Come to think of it, there haven't been any. Care to remedy the gap in my manly education. No? Oh, well . . .' his mocking smile faded into a speculative appraisal. 'I should have guessed, you know. Only a virgin could be so supremely confident of her physical invulnerability, so contemptuous of male weaknesses. You've never been truly awakened to your own frailties, never put yourself completely at the mercy of your passions. Just you wait, Jess, until someone comes along to light a fire in your guts. All your defiant certainties will melt like wax.'

'The hell they will!' Jessica fought free of the compelling tug of his words, afraid to face the possibility of their truth. 'I want my nightgowns back.'

'Well, you're not getting them. The nearest you'll get to white from now on is distinctly off.' He leant down to fossick through the froth in the box and drew out a cream-coloured lace see-through top and a miniscule pair of matching panties. 'Just make sure Kristin gets an eyeful of you in this.'

'I can't wear that!' Jessica was torn between horror and traitorous laughter. She had never gone for such little-girl looks, they were absurd on a woman of her height. Still, she couldn't help her hand going out and catching the drift of lace as Matthew let it fall. It *was* beautiful, and obviously extremely expensive. But really . . .

'I thought these things went out in the fifties,' she murmured. 'A baby doll! The last time I saw one of these was in an old Doris Day movie on TV. Do women actually *wear* these things? And maribou—!' she ran the feathery trim through her fingers, '—honestly Matt, what on earth made you get it? You didn't really imagine that I'd wear it.'

He gave her such a black scowl that she was taken aback. 'Some women find sexy nightwear erotic,' he said sarcastically.

Here was her chance to extract a little revenge.

'I can't imagine why, it's so . . . *adolescent*. Anyone who found this erotic would have to be a case of arrested development. Oh!' She put her hand over her mouth and widened her eyes mischievously at him. 'Do *you*? Oh, Matt, that does date you a bit, doesn't it?' She giggled and held up the lace in front of her, smoothing it down over her curves and affecting a lispy voice. 'Do you like playing wif pwetty baby dollies, Maffew?'

To her glee he went dark red and growled at her. 'Any moment, Jessica, I'm going to put you over my knee.'

'Daddy smack pwetty dolly?' she pouted at him and put her thumb in her mouth. 'Make pwetty dolly cry? Ouf——!' as he launched off the couch and sprang over the coffee table to haul her against his chest.

'You shouldn't have said that, Jessica, just what are you trying to do?'

'I don't know what you mean,' she gasped, shaken by the speed of his attack.

'Oh yes you do. You like provoking me. You do it

all the time. Have you discovered a new form? Do you think that now we've exchanged secrets about sex you can tease me with your body, too? You must have a hell of a trust in yourself . . . or in me.'

Jessica was stricken. Surely he couldn't think . . .? 'Matt, I'm sorry,' she said, appalled at her thoughtlessness. 'I wasn't teasing you about, you know, about Lisa.' She cleared her throat and pushed against him, her hands catching in the wispy maribou as she tilted her head to look gravely into his eyes. 'I would never——'

He cut her off with an impatient sound. 'I know that, Jess, you don't even have to say it. God forbid that you should have to pick and choose your words for fear of offending me. I much prefer you spontaneous; even when you're insulting me I know that you would never deliberately fling that in my face . . . you have too much integrity.' His eyes dropped to her mouth as she moved restively against him.

'I suppose I did get a bit carried away, though,' she admitted nervously. 'You can let me go, now, Matt.'

'Sssshh!' He pulled her face into the warmth of his shirt-front so that she missed the calculating gleam that lit his eyes. 'It's Kent and Kristin, I think they're back.'

'Let me go.' Jessica wriggled to no avail.

'No, don't. This is our chance to do a little extra convincing.' He bent his head but Jessica jerked her face away.

'No——'

'Don't be stupid, Jess. It's what they'd expect. Unless, of course, you want this all to drag on for longer. Kiss me for God's sake and lets get this over with.'

His rasping impatience convinced her, that and the implication that she *wanted* to remain in his house. Jessica strained to hear footsteps, the sound of the spare key in the door. Instead, all she heard was the thunder of blood in her veins as her mind was flooded with sensations.

He kissed her long and sweet and slow, and, as he felt her body soften against him, his arms loosened and he lifted his mouth to brush it in a gentling caress across her proud cheekbones, the sweeping curve of her chin, and the faint uptilt at the corners of her mouth. Then he was delving into the moist depths again, his lips hard yet soft, slanting across hers as he sought for access. His hand stroked to her chin and he tugged at it, parting her lips further, his cheek rasping lightly against her own. His hand moved to her throat, fondling the long curve, his fingers stroking against her pulsebeats, the pads of his thumbs sensitive to her soaring excitement.

Automatically Jessica slid her arms around his neck, swaying into the lean body as she fed his hungry mouth. His hands moved down again, feeling their way across her body, moving from back to waist to hip, softly massaging the rounded cheeks of her bottom through the thin jersey of her dress. As she felt the stirring of his desire against her stomach she gave one last thought to where they were . . . and why.

'Are they here——?'

'Nearly.' He smothered her choked gasp with his hot mouth. 'Just a little bit longer.' His tongue slid between her teeth as he gripped her even more tightly against him.

Jessica felt a melting from within as a hot core of passion welled, pulsing through her body. She was scarcely aware of moving with him, of sinking, until she felt the cool slippery press of leather against her back as Matt followed her on to the couch, half-leaning, half-lying over her. Muttering against her mouth he pulled the lacy nightdress from where it was trapped between them, slinging it on to the floor before his hand returned to slip the pearl-buttons of her shirt-waister loose from their anchors.

His mouth paused from its explorations as he pushed aside the jersey and drew a deep breath at the sight of her breasts nestling roundly within the peach camisole. The lace trim glided over their upper curves while below two soft points pressed against the smooth sheen of satin.

'Pretty,' Matthew murmured in a husky voice, tasting the bared skin, brushing aside the strap of her camisole with his lips, licking his way down the inner curve of her arm. Jessica's hands slipped through his dark locks as she lay trembling, astounded at the storm of feeling he was arousing. Was this what he had meant about being at the mercy of passion? It didn't make her feel uncertain, it made her feel fabulously, gloriously *certain*. She felt like a woman, a beautiful, desirable woman ... the only woman in the world, soaring high, everything she could ever want encompassed in her arms. She watched through heavy, half-closed lids as Matthew introduced her to new delights, exposed nerve endings she never knew she had.

He bared one breast with a sweep of his hand, studying the beautiful conformation with slow appreciation. His face was slightly flushed, dark hair falling over his brow where Jessica had ruffled it. His breath had acquired an unsteady rasp and his mouth a sensual fullness from its erotic quest. Jessica could feel the tension in his muscles, smell the faintly spicy scent of his maleness.

'Pretty,' he murmured again, raising a finger to stroke against the soft, flat pink disc that crested the rise of her breast. 'Like a velvety rose petal.'

Jessica clutched at his shoulders. His mouth was so close to her skin she could feel his breath like hot licks of fire. Her nipple tingled and reacted with startling, almost painful suddenness, rising to beg his attention.

His eyes lifted to meet hers, and she saw they were black and hot and steamy, and she was glad.

'Not a petal,' he whispered in soft praise, 'a rose-hip . . . fruit of the rose. Do you taste as sweet as the fragrant scent of you, I wonder . . .'

Jessica cried out as he slid a cupping hand beneath the puckering sweet and, lifting, sipped at her. A great gush of feeling cascaded through her body as he sucked at her pale flesh, baring the other breast and feasting there also. She couldn't believe she could feel such pleasure and still live, She moaned and arched her body against him, moving restlessly to try and assuage the ache that was gathering between her thighs.

'Oh God, yes . . . it feels good, doesn't it, Jess, so good,' he groaned as her hip pushed against his swollen hardness. His mouth returned to hers as his hands touched her, healing the pain that the absence of his lips and tongue caused in her taut breasts. Jessica ran her hands down the hardness of his ribs, pulling the shirt free from his waistband to slide underneath to feel the hot dryness of his back.

'Yes . . . touch me,' he rasped, hips pressing her more deeply into the soft cushions, 'God, I hope you want me as much as I want you.' He bit gently at her throat and as she turned her head she saw the little pile of lace trailing on the floor.

'You . . . lied,' she slurred, her tongue so large and heavy in her mouth that she could hardly speak. While her body moved only languidly, inside everything was working at double rate as sensation piled on sensation.

'No touch me . . . see how much,' he pulled her hand intimately against the apex of his thighs and Jessica felt a jolt of passionate apprehension.

'I . . . mean . . . Kent and Kristin.' She managed to

push him sideways so that she could squirm against the back if the couch. She lay there panting, her hands braced against his chest. She had no idea how much time had passed ... minutes ... hours ... days! Their legs were still entangled and she could feel the pulsing heat of his arousal sapping her weak resistance. Her eyes were wide, dazed, tinged with a kind of astonishment that was almost a seduction in itself. 'They're not here ... you just said that——' she gave a tiny choking cry as Matthew leaned forward and gently kissed her where a tiny patch of freckles salted her collarbone. '—you just said that to trick me into ...' She faltered as he smiled lazily, making no effort to get her back into his arms, just looking at her body with a sensual satisfaction.

'... into what, darling? Into something you didn't want to do? Oh, Jessica, virgins shouldn't tell such whopping lies. You were having a lovely time ... mmm? Besides, would I do that to you? Of course they're here.'

And they were. Jessica heard the door open as he spoke. She tried to rear up off the couch but Matt grabbed her with one hand, while with the other he prevented her from pulling together the edges of her dress.

He didn't let her struggle free until Kent and Kristin were actually in the room, then he casually rolled off the couch to face his guests with an expression of masculine triumph that reinforced the scene they had just witnessed.

'Excuse us for interrupting,' Kent joked, to Jessica's unutterable embarrassment. 'I suppose having guests is cramping your style a bit.'

'Only a very little,' Matthew replied smoothly. 'Jessica was just thanking me for a little present I got her. Here, darling,' he gathered up the debris, 'why don't you go and slip into something more comfortable?'

Mortified Jessica snatched the box and stormed out in silent outrage. Kristin, however, caught up with her in the hallway.

'Don't be embarrassed,' she said kindly. 'Matt always did come on rather strong. He's very highly sexed.'

So, she was beginning to be afraid, was Jessica. 'I'm not embarrassed,' she denied stiffly.

'You were as red as a traffic light. Matt, on the other hand, wasn't fazed at all. Maybe he's getting bored with you already. Enjoy him while you can, Jessie, because I don't think you're going to have him much longer.'

'Really,' said Jessica icily, halting at the door of her room, dying to go in and sink her burning body into the cool sheets.

'Really. He's just using you, like he uses every other woman. But not me. He was in love with me . . . and he will be again. So if I were you, I'd squirrel away a bit of insurance—you're going to need it in the very near future.'

Jessica's face was stiff with the effort of keeping it blank, though she was sickened by the other woman's monumental stupidity. She actually believed that she was irresistible, that she could get Matt merely because she wanted him.

'I don't think so,' she said, with quiet confidence. 'I've got a few years on you Kristin, you'd be much wiser to hold on to what you have rather than try and compete with me. You might be more beautiful, but mere beauty no longer satisfies Matt—he wants a mind as well as a body. You could never meet him as an equal, never get him but by playing elaborate games. He only *thinks* he's using me. He doesn't know it yet, but he's in love with me. He's more mine than he ever was yours.' And God forgive her for her lies, but it was worth it to see the angry bafflement on Kristin's face at her calmness.

'We'll see about that!' Kristin's voice was shrill with suppressed rage, her eyes blue stones in her lovely face. 'I could take him away from you like *that*!' She snapped her fingers. 'You're just a novelty at the moment—all that junk about being equals! Matt doesn't want an equal, he wants a *woman*. And he's always liked his women feminine. He can't stand pushy broads. I wouldn't be surprised if he isn't stringing you along just for the pleasure of teaching you who's boss!'

Jessica slid her door shut with a snap, masking the twisted jealousy on the other side. Her heart was pounding and her palms felt clammy. She threw the box in her hands violently on to the bed and went over to slam the sliding door between the two rooms completely closed.

Was that why Matt had tried to make love to her, because she was a novelty? Had he been titillated by her confession of virginity? She held her head between her hands and rocked distractedly. Think, Jessica, think. Don't let a desperate, bitter woman manipulate you.

They had been on the couch for a long time, so he *had* tricked her . . . but she had fallen for it gratefully, she had wanted him. And though she had pushed him away before the Farrows arrived she had expected him to take her back into his arms, to overcome her resistance. *Overcome?* What was she saying? Jessica was aghast at herself. Was there, beneath her independent skin, a 'little woman' screaming to get out? She shuddered. No! But Matt *had* aroused that reckless taste for danger that she had tried so hard to bury since that night when they had met. To make love with him would be dangerously exciting, tonight had proved it—he was so skilful, experienced . . . and the sense of danger gave their passion its extra edge. She had drawn back, wanting but afraid . . .

remembering where her last bout of recklessness had taken her.

And Matt? His desire had been real enough, gloriously real. He had been faster to control himself, to turn the situation to his own advantage, but that he was aroused had still been embarrassingly obvious. Jessica went hot at the memory. Had she looked like that too—flushed and achingly unsatisfied? She certainly had proof now that he had overcome his sexual problem.

Jessica frowned as she got ready for bed, shunning the tempting box of fripperies in favour of her own camisole and panties. As she was beginning to know Matt better, a weird protective instinct was over-growing her intitial animosity. It was all right for Jessica to try to thwart him, to plot against him, but she hated the idea of that spiteful snake of a woman doing the same. And she did believe at least one thing that she had told Kristin. Matt did need a woman who was his equal, a woman whom he could respect as well as desire, if he was to sustain a long-term relationship. Matt's much-professed dislike of aggressive women seemed to Jessica another symptom of that unattractive self-protective behaviour of his. He was unwilling, or unable, to admit that a vital part of him admired such women. They threatened his own sense of independ-ence, because if he were to form a relationship with an intelligent, articulate woman he might actually want to make it permanent. He might actually fall in love and want to get married . . . and risk being hurt all over again.

Jessica drifted off to sleep pondering her analysis. It didn't occur to her that the same criteria might actually be applied to herself . . . and was being, in the very next room. If she *had* examined her own prejudices and attitudes she might very well have been horrified at her smug self-deception.

Telling herself that she would have protected the devil himself from a witch like Kristin, Jessica played her part to the hilt over the next two days. Only there was no trying to beat her at her own game. Jessica was herself—strong and confident. Matt seemed first amused, then complacent about her change of tune, but Jessica refused to let it annoy her. She would show them all that she was thoroughly in control. She no longer panicked when he touched her ... after all, they had done a great deal more than just touch the other night, but she couldn't deny the sensual surge that occurred each time it happened. And knowing that, Jessica felt physically sick at her new, purely instinctual appreciation of the private hell Matt had endured in his marriage. How would Jessica have felt if Matt had laughed at her inexperience on that couch, had taunted her that she wasn't woman enough to arouse him! It would have been devastatingly humiliating. No wonder Matt had been so grimly determined to cleanse his life of Lisa's twisted presence, to tear himself free at any cost. To accept his failure as a husband was a bitter pill to swallow, but to accept failure as a man would have utterly destroyed him.

The strain of coping with her rapidly shifting feelings, of masking them under calm composure, took its toll on Jessica. One night, when they all went out to dinner at a popular, crowded Italian restaurant, Jessica decided that for once she would try to enjoy herself for the sake of it, rather than to impress anyone else. Hell, even slaves had time off occasionally.

She ate and drank liberally, aware—and not caring—that Kent Farrow seemed slightly surprised at her sudden gay frivolity. Matt didn't stint on the red wine either, since he had left the white Corniche at home, preferring to walk the short distance to the

restaurant in spite of Kristin's complaints about what
it would do to her fragile gold evening sandals.

Unaccustomed as she was to alcohol, it went straight
to Jessica's head. If it hadn't, no doubt she would have
declined the offer from a strange, but personally brash
young man to join the jostling mass on the dance floor.
Without even looking at Matt, Jessica leapt to her feet
and for what seemed like hours was swept from one
partner after another until, to her surprise, she found
herself dancing with Kent Farrow, who had to tilt his
head upwards to talk to her.

'You don't have to do this you know.'

'I beg your pardon?' The noise was beginning to
make Jessica's ears ache and she felt quite hot in her
thin, strapless gown.

Kent moved his mouth closer to her ear and raised
his voice. 'I said you don't have to do this, not with
Matt. It's only necessary to see the way he looks at you
to know he'd never look twice at another woman. If
ever I doubted his intentions towards my wife the way
he's glaring at me over her shoulder would have laid
my fears to rest. I know Kristin's behaved badly, but
don't let it spoil what you have with Matt.'

'I——' at that moment Kent swung her around to
avoid another couple and Jessica found herself staring
straight into Matt's eyes. She shivered and time
telescoped. He had exactly the same expression on his
face as he had had at that party in Auckland.

'There's a proverb, Jessica: a man who marries a
woman of uncommon beauty is courting anxiety and
danger. That's true, even without the marriage bit. A
man in love is prey to insecurities enough without
having jealousy deliberately thrust upon him.'

Matt, in love? Jessica nearly laughed, nearly cried.

'Matt's not in love with me,' she blurted out.

'Passion, desire, there are many ways of being in
love.' Kent the bluff, hearty rough-diamond was

revealing a sensitivity that surprised Jessica. She was ashamed that she had dismissed him so lightly because of his unfortunate choice of wife. 'There's what Kristin and I have ... I married her at fifty and she gave me a new lease of life. I know she likes excitement, attention, admiration, but more than all those she needs security. She's not like you, independent and free-spirited, she arouses a man's protective instinct. She's not always like this, you know. She has a lot of good qualities, but she's afraid. She's thirty next month, a painful milestone for any woman, but especially one like Kristin, who believes all her attraction lies in her physical beauty. Seeing you, seeing how Matt admires you even though you're not beautiful as she is, is difficult for her. She feels everything slipping through her fingers ... believe me, I know the feeling and I'm going to do everything I can to help her through it.'

Jessica rested her head against the side of his as they danced, suddenly feeling sorry, unbearably sorry for Kent, for his difficult, neurotically afraid wife, and for herself. God, she was becoming maudlin and her head was beginning to thump.

It was with relief that she followed him back to the table and there heard Matt's terse suggestion that they leave. Kristin looked daggers at her all the way home and Jessica realised with a touch of weary hysteria that she thought Jessica was now trying to move in on her husband. Poor Kristin, she really *was* insecure.

In a strained atmosphere they all settled down to coffee and liqueurs in the lounge, Jessica accepting a Kahlua and milk on the assumption that it was too late to try and sober up this evening. She hadn't a clue what the conversation was about but gradually she became aware that Matt had stopped ignoring her. He was slightly drunk, she realised, and slightly insulting with it. Kristin's delight in the further deterioration of the evening made Jessica even more slightly insulting in return.

The final straw came when Matt brought out fresh drinks, and there was none for Jessica.

'Where's mine? I wanted another Kahlua.'

'I think you've had enough, don't you? You have trouble enough controlling yourself when you're sober,' he said cuttingly.

'I am perfectly sober,' said Jessica in icy reply. 'I'm sure you'll agree. Because if I wasn't I might get nasty, I might start blurting out things I shouldn't.'

They glared at each other, not even looking around as Kristin peeped: 'What kind of things?'

'Deep, dark, secrets,' said Jessica tauntingly. 'Should I tell her, Matt, darling?'

'Go ahead,' he said coolly, but Jessica could see the strained muscle shift over his jaw.

'Well,' she said, the knowledge that he was furious egging her on. 'The truth is ...' she sucked in a breath, 'Matt beats me!'

'Now that is amazing—I thought it was the other way around,' Kent laughed. Jessica knew he was trying to lighten the leaden atmosphere but it was definitely the wrong thing to say.

Jessica sought feebly for a reply, but as she opened her mouth it was snapped shut as she was hauled to her feet.

'If you'll excuse us, Kent, Kristin,' said Matt through his teeth, polite even in extremity.

'Where on earth are you going?' Kristin's blue eyes were annoyed that she was going to miss the showdown.

'To give her the beating she deserves, what else? Good night. Say "good night", Jessica.'

'Good night,' said Jessica in stunned obedience and allowed herself to be dragged along to the big room at the end of the house.

'Matt, what are you doing? What's going on?'

'Exactly what I told Kristin.' He grabbed Jessica's judogi from where it was neatly folded on the bench against the wall and thrust the garments into her hand. 'Put them on.'

'Don't be ridiculous, Matt,' she cried, as it dawned on her what he meant to do.

'Put them on. By God, Jessica, we're going to settle this once and for all.' He began to pull off his clothes, reaching for his own, similarly folded costume. Jessica quickly turned her back, her breathing unsteady.

'Don't be silly. We can't fight. You're drunk.'

'So are you. That makes us even. What's wrong? Scared you can't beat me even when I'm drunk and incapable?' He came around in front of her, swiftly tying the belt of his jacket. 'So the Amazon isn't so sure of herself after all. Did I light a fire in your guts, sweetheart?'

She almost attacked him there and then, even though she knew this was wrong, that he was deliberately goading her. Angrily she stormed off into the sauna room and dragged off her filmy blue dress. She wasn't wearing a bra and the jacket of her judogi slid like cool fingers across her skin.

'I'll show him,' she muttered as she tightened her belt, not sure what it was exactly she wanted to show him.

She went out, trying not to look too closely at him in the loose white jacket and pants. He was just an opponent, like any other. Unfortunately her tongue wasn't obeying her brain.

'Now, Matt. Would you mind telling me before we begin what all this macho rubbish is about?'

He was standing, primed for action, in the middle of the mat, all sullen eyes and angry mouth. 'I thought you didn't like draping yourself over men? You did a damned good imitation of it tonight. What were you

trying to do? Embarrass me? Turn on every man in
the joint? You did both pretty successfully. Or
perhaps you were lifting their wallets, along with
their——'

'I am not a thief,' Jessica yelled at him over her
pounding headache, cutting off that last, crude,
reference.

'You stole from *me*.' She could see that he had
worked himself into a rage and was coldly intent on
maintaining it.

'The one and only time.'

'But you still haven't learnt your lesson ... *still*.'
His voice was thick, gorged with an emotion that
Jessica couldn't read. Hate? Contempt? 'Come on,
Jessica, you're only wasting time. Fight me. Come on.
I *dare* you.'

In her overconfident state the naked taunt was
enough. Automatically Jessica slid into a defensive
posture as she circled him warily, her mind dropping
to a deeper level of concentration, breathing slowing,
balance constant. She tried to relax so that she could
react instinctively to each opening as it occurred. The
first tentative grips and twists were a testing time,
each opponent exploring the other's defences, seeking
the weak points.

Inebriated as they were, they could still appreciate
each other's skill. Matt's physical strength was greater,
but in judo that wasn't necessarily an advantage and
Jessica wasn't intimidated by his aggressive attacking.
He was angry and anger allied to his alcohol-slowed
reactions whittled away any advantage he had.

For a long time the only sound in the big room was
the sound of roughened breathing, the quiet slap of
bare feet against the vinyl mat, the faint grunts that
accompanied a successful throw. The falls became
fewer as they tired and more and more an attack ended
in a stalemate. Jessica's skin was slick with sweat, the

loose silken jacket beginning to cling. Her hair, which had been piled on top of her head when they started, had long since tumbled and flew about her shoulders as she ducked and darted.

Matt's jacket had been half pulled from its tie and his smooth, muscular, almost hairless chest gleamed like oiled satin. Panting, Jessica found her concentration failing as she gripped his lapels, her hands sliding against his perspiring chest. He blocked her move and tried a counter move of his own. Jessica felt the bunching of muscles in his arms and thighs and instinct told her what he was trying to do almost before he began the move. As he turned slightly to his left, attempting to break her balance for a hip throw, she quickly shifted her hips and checked his move briefly with her left hand on his right hip. Using his own momentum she very neatly effected a throw on the reverse side. He hit the mat with a wooshing breath and swivelled, pushing backwards. But instead of springing to his feet he caught Jessica's leg just behind her ankle with one of his feet and brought the sole of his other foot to press firmly just under her knee. Jessica fell like a young sapling, straight on to her back. Incredibly, she felt almost as much exhilaration at being the victim of an expert throw as she did at bringing off a move of her own. He was good. Very good. Before she could move he was on top of her, attempting an arm lock.

Limbs weighted by tiredness, they grappled for a few minutes, neither gaining ascendancy. Anger had long been drained away by the intense physical exertion. Jessica's hands seemed suddenly unable to grip, sliding over his silky jacket. She could feel the damp heat of his bare chest against the gaping V of her own jacket. The air felt heavy, oppressive in her nostrils, musky with sweat. Slowly, inexorably, the battle of bodies was becoming something else. Their limbs slid in slow motion against each other until each hold was almost a caress, a stroking, easily broken grip that invited a counter-caress.

When his arm moved against her throat in the classic lock it was only a light brush, pushing up his loose sleeve so that the soft, dark brown hairs on his forearm whispered across her fiery skin. Somehow Jessica's hand slid inside his jacket, feeling the ridged outlines of his ribs. He murmured something and moved his head, and they were kissing, their tongues continuing a secret love-battle of their own under cover of the joined mouths.

Matt eased himself sideways off her and they rolled on to their sides, hips moving against each other, arms locked at waist-level. Matt made no effort to slide his hands under her loose top, but he didn't have to. Through the thin, slippery material he could feel her breasts swell against his chest, feel every line and nerve of her as if she was completely naked in his arms. He groaned and rocked her against his pelvis.

Jessica closed her eyes against the bright lights of the gym, a pyrotechnic explosion taking place inside her skull. Her earlier headache and lethargy had been replaced by an almost super-sensitised clarity of mind, every vibration of breath and movement heightened to an incredible degree. Matt slid his leg between hers, pushing it against the juncture of her thighs so that her body arched with the electric contact. She tried to squirm impossibly closer and his hands fell on to her hips, holding her still as he bit her gently on the neck, and she gave a half sob as she felt the hot pulse of his groin against her. Her breasts ached with a new fullness, her belly with an emptiness that she despaired of filling.

'I think we've just given the sport a new dimension,' came the grating husky voice in her ear, followed by the erotic probe of his tongue. 'God, if only I wasn't so drunk.'

With difficulty Jessica raised her head from his throat, resting sweat-darkened hair against the soft cushion of vinyl. Slowly, the tension drained out of her body, leaving her feeling strangely enervated.

'Who won?' she asked stumblingly.

'I'm not sure. I think we'd better call it a draw.'

'Until next time.'

He laughed softly. 'Never give up, do you? Neither do I.'

'Want to start all over again?'

'I'd love to, but frankly, Jess——' he yawned hugely, 'I feel wiped out.'

Jessica was both piqued and relieved. Her own body felt too much like gelatine. She didn't even want to move, just lie here, curled warmly in his arms, at peace with herself and him. She knew that if both had been stone cold sober they wouldn't be doing this . . . and if they had been only slightly less than sober they would now be making love. Regretfully, she allowed him to pull her to her unsteady feet. When she would have moved away he stopped her, a hand splaying along her jaw, saying out loud what they had both been thinking.

'I want you.' His voice was gritty from tiredness and the dregs of desire. 'But when I take you I want to be able to remember it in the morning. Tonight I'd be liable to fall asleep on you.'

Jessica almost blurted out that she wouldn't mind.

'When? You mean *if*, don't you?' she said defensively.

He smiled, a thoroughly wicked smile that tightened the muscles of her stomach. 'What if I dare you?'

She tossed her head, the sweat on her body beginning to cool as her brain began to function again.

'I'm not so reckless that I can't see through a typically masculine ploy like that one.'

'Oh, but you are ... very, very reckless,' he said knowingly. 'You offered, didn't you, to break into my house? Your brother isn't the kind of man who would have wanted you to take that risk. Why did he let you?'

'He couldn't very well stop me, with a broken leg,' Jessica answered cautiously. It was the first time, since Auckland, that he had asked her about that night. Did it mean that he was now prepared to listen to her side?

'Knowing what you're like he probably couldn't stop you anyway,' he said drily. 'You're too damned determined for your own good ... and your brother is too damned soft for his.'

Soft? An odd word to use about somebody you had planned to mercilessly crush. 'He loves Fiona ... but he was so desperate, so confused. Lisa had told him so much about your ruthlessness that he just wasn't thinking straight,' she said, putting everything she had into convincing him.

'Then it's a pity he didn't take the time to straighten himself out, isn't it? It would have saved us all grief. Why didn't he just bloody well sit tight?'

'Because you were going to——' Jessica broke off, staring at him. This time his frustration took on a different aspect, as an incredible thought occurred to her. 'Oh my God!'

His eyes narrowed at her stunned whisper, and his face shuttered as she went on. 'You weren't,' she breathed, reaching for the certainty, 'you weren't going to use them in court, you never intended to. You didn't want the publicity any more than Carl did. You only wanted to make her settle, to bluff her into settling *before* you went into court.'

'Is that what you think?' he asked, giving nothing away.

'I ... I don't know ...' It was what she *wanted* to think, so badly that she couldn't face it logically. If only he would tell her ...

Matthew watched her struggle with conflicting emotions. He refused to help her. Pride dictated that she be allowed to reach her own conclusions. Trust had to be wholehearted, or it wasn't worth having. He knew he shouldn't expect her to be able to judge him fairly without all the facts but the need was in him to force her to choose between instinct and logic. He wanted her to choose him in spite of the weight of the evidence. It wasn't fair, but it was necessary to him.

'*Were* you bluffing? Like you did over that locked door?' As the words passed her lips Jessica became aware of the wider implications ... the tantalising possibilities. 'But ... if you were bluffing *then*, two years ago, you must have been bluffing this time, too. Then what am I doing here? If I *had* refused to come, what would you have done? Nothing?' She was more confused than ever now. 'Why am I here!'

'You tell me. What *are* you doing here, Jess?' he asked softly, not confirming or denying, only forcing her mind into ever-diminishing circles. 'Could it be that you liked meeting up with someone as strong as you? That you *wanted* to be forced into coming? Think about it, Jess. Maybe the prospect of defeat is what you find exciting in life, not the desire for victory. Maybe you're here now because you wondered what it would be like to fight with all your might and yet still be conquered, still be won. Is that what your silent challenge is, Jess?'

CHAPTER NINE

'HERE'S to success, may the new Australian Electronic Industries have a long and profitable future!' Kent's long-stemmed crystal glass caught the light as he lifted it towards the centre of the long dining table.

'Success,' murmured Jessica, raising her glass also and smiling at the craggy, contented face. Matt, clinking his glass against hers, sought her eyes but she looked carefully away. Ever since their erotic bout in the exercise room the day before yesterday Jessica had struggled to maintain a calm front, uneasily aware that Matt was watching and waiting ... for what she wasn't sure. Her emotions had been quite thoroughly shaken up, and she wasn't sure any more what she believed. Was Matt the ruthless opportunist she had originally thought him to be? Or the vulnerable man he had revealed to her in quieter moments?

And what about that final provocative suggestion ... that she was subconsciously inviting him to conquer her? Bluff or not, had some primitive part of her mind contributed to her downfall ... not *wanting* to find a way out of his trap until she had tested herself against him?

'Come on, Jess, you've hardly touched your champagne.' The velvety voice slithered down her neck. 'It's the best, Dom Perignon, and you can have as many glasses as you wish tonight, I promise I won't beat you.'

Still refusing to look at him Jessica took a tiny, cautious taste. They had dressed up for this celebratory dinner—Matt in the black and white that suited him so well. Out of the corner of her eye she could see that he looked sleek and darkly handsome. Both men looked buoyant, as well they might. Over the past two days the minor differences that had been holding up the negotiations had been magically smoothed away. Jessica didn't know how much influence her tipsy behaviour and Matt's angry response had had, but Kent had definitely seemed more relaxed and forthcoming since then. In fact he seemed to have gained in stature, rather than been diminished, by his decision to deal with the younger man. Perhaps even he himself had not realised how the pressures of age and work had been combining to affect him.

Kristin seemed different, too, tonight. For a start she was dressed almost modestly in a simple white cowl-necked dress that made her look feminine and fragile and more beautiful than Jessica had ever seen her. Her skin was smooth and faintly flushed, her eyes glittered with repressed excitement. Her nervous lustre gave Jessica vague forebodings, though on the surface everything seemed normal.

Kristin in white contrasted dramatically with Jessica in black. She had worn every other dress in her wardrobe, except this one and she *had* to wear something different on tonight of all nights, she had convinced herself. She should have destroyed the thing but it had been expensive and it was beautiful, so it wasn't surprising that Jill had packed it.

That Matt recognised it was obvious from the hissing breath he drew when she joined the others in the lounge before dinner. For a moment something dangerous had flickered in his dark eyes but then he had merely raised his eyebrows with a quizzical amusement, that made her grit her teeth.

'Well, Matt, in spite of all the obstacles I've enjoyed my stay,' Kent leaned back in his chair benignly. 'Kristin has, too, haven't you, pet? Thanks to your

Jessica's company. As soon as we sign that agreement officially tomorrow and issue a press statement, we'll have to think about moving on. I've promised Kristin a long holiday, so we'll go back to Melbourne so that I can tie up some loose ends, then it's off to Bali for a few weeks.' Kristin's life was one long holiday, thought Jessica sourly as Kent continued. 'It's thanks to industries like ours, Matt, that I can keep in touch with all my investments wherever I am in the world. So Kristin can't complain I'm neglecting her, and my directors can't complain I'm neglecting them. You ought to try a bit more delegation yourself . . . I'm sure Jessica would appreciate seeing more of you.'

'I thought all your business talk was over,' Kristin pouted, her midnight hair gleaming like coal under the rice-paper shades. 'Can't we talk about something more exciting?'

'What do you suggest?' asked Kent, with a fond smile.

Fashion or gossip, thought Jessica, and was flabbergasted when the answer came.

'What about babies?' Kristin preened at their astonishment.

'What about babies?' asked Jessica faintly.

'I'm going to have one.'

Jessica stared with her mouth open. The two men came to life, suddenly looking at Kristin as if a halo had appeared above her head.

'A baby? A baby?' Kent's face was a picture of wonder mingled with pride. 'Our baby! Are you sure?'

Kristin lowered her lovely eyes, the picture of a gentle Madonna. '*I'm* sure. I haven't confirmed it officially yet, I thought I'd leave it until we got back to Melbourne.'

Jessica was extremely suspicious. Was she or wasn't she? Was this just another way of getting everyone's attention?

'How far ... I mean how long ...?' Kent gabbled excitedly, acting more like a teenager than a middle-aged man.

'About eight weeks, I think,' Kristin replied. Her blue eyes shifted vaguely. 'I think it must have happened about the time we came up for those preliminary talks of yours. Remember, Kent, you had to cut them short and fly out to Perth and then I stayed on for some shopping?'

Jessica froze while the two men shook hands and kissed Kristin and exchanged joking remarks about heirs. There was smug triumph all over Kristin's face and when her eyes met Jessica's they were like blue stones, shiny and hard. Oh yes, she was pregnant all right and she had just opened the cellar door nice and wide. Jessica didn't for an instant believe that Kristin and Matt had ever renewed that old love affair ... but would her husband? Such a suggestion would not only destroy any hopes of that agreement being signed tomorrow but it would also tear apart three lives ... four if she counted herself, thought Jessica with wrenching pain. Was Kristin mad enough to do it? What was she going to do? Make a scene now? Blurt out her sick fantasies?

'Are you feeling all right?' Kent was asking anxiously. 'Perhaps you shouldn't be trudging around the city on these shopping expeditions. Perhaps we ought to put off Bali.'

'Let's wait and see what the doctor says,' said Kristin calmly and Jessica swallowed her relief. She was obviously still going to hedge her bets. Her heart thumped again when Kristin said to Matt, 'You look almost as tickled as Kent. Would you like to have children, Matt?'

'I would have had four by now, if Lisa had been willing,' he smiled, and there was an ironic twist to his mouth that made the smile bitter.

'I think this calls for another bottle of champagne, don't you?' said Kent, finishing off his glass. 'I can't believe it, it's like a wish come true. What made you change your mind, Kristy?' as Matt went to fetch another bottle.

Kristin smiled, cat-like, and gave an elegant little shrug. 'I thought it was time, that's all.'

Matt came back, followed by the Hos, who offered the couple polite congratulations.

Jessica hid a smile at Kim's: 'I hope Mr Farrow's wife will be very happy.' Kristin thought her manner of address was quaint, not seeing it as the subtle way the young Vietnamese woman put her in her place. Kristin's casual disdain for the hired help and propensity for losing her temper when something wasn't done exactly to her satifaction hadn't endeared her to Kim. Kim had made a point of serving her with inscrutable efficiency, reserving all her shy warmth and giggling charm for Jessica. Kristin was firmly relegated to a position of wife of an honoured guest, while Jessica was treated as an integral part of the household.

Perhaps I'm just jealous, Jessica thought as she dutifully toasted the parents-to-be. She had never had very much to do with children, never felt any strong maternal urge. Her eyes wandered to Matthew. Of course, she had never been so in love with a man that she wanted to have his children. Matt was looking down at the slow rise of bubbles in his glass, his face guarded. What would his children be like? Little devils probably. He would try and order them around like a personal regiment and they, having inherited his impossible genes, would resist, no doubt from the moment they were capable of speech.

He looked up at that moment, and saw her wry smile.

'What are you thinking?'

'I'm thinking that if you had children the first word they would probably say would be "no".'

'Not Mama or Daddy?'

Jessica shook her head. 'Not assertive enough.'

He chuckled. 'And your children, I suppose, would be little angels of obedience.'

'Of course, they would inherit their mother's even temper.'

'Even your temper,' he agreed, 'not to mention your sheer cussedness.' Their eyes met, brimming with silent and oddly tender laughter.

'What beautiful timing,' Kent was saying. 'Here I was thinking I was about to embark on the biggest deal of my life and I find instead that I've got an even bigger one in the pipeline.' He couldn't stop grinning, looking from one to the other as if to confirm his good fortune in their eyes. If he got any more puffed up, he was going to explode, thought Jessica. How magnificently Kristin had garnered the limelight. These two men had spent weeks hammering out an agreement that would rationalise an entire Australian industry yet their achievement had been very neatly put into the shade by the unconfirmed existence of a microscopic collection of cells.

'Well, now you've disposed of the one you can concentrate on the other,' she said and received a mild admonishment from Matt.

'You should know better than that, Jess. Signing the actual deal is only a beginning. Once the details are released we'll be bombarded with red tape. No doubt some of our competitors will run to the government screaming "monopoly". This cross-shareholding is going to give us a huge potential for growth, and there'll be those who would love to see us knocked back.'

'Is there a chance that might happen?' asked Jessica, aware that her small-business experience ill-equipped her to understand the ramifications of million-dollar deals.

'Not if I have anything to do with it,' Matt replied with a supreme confidence that had Kent chuckling.

'And he will, he will. Back-to-back, eh, Matt, we can fight off all comers.'

Kristin began to cry. Jewel-like tears slid prettily down her face and she once more became the focus of attention.

'I'm sorry,' she sniffed, 'I just don't know what is the matter with me.'

Her husband was all gentle solicitude. 'It's all right, Kristy, we understand. You're bound to be a bit emotional. Why don't you come and lie down for a while? Pregnant ladies need a bit of pampering.'

'How much more pampered can she get?' murmured Jessica under her breath as Kent led his wife protectively away. Matt, who had got to his feet, gave her a sharp look as he subsided.

There was silence for a few minutes, while Matt twisted his glass in lean fingers. 'I wonder what kind of life that kid will have,' he said idly.

'Well, it's starting off with a lot of advantages— Kent'll make sure his son or daughter has only the best.'

'The best that money can buy, yes. But what about the things that money can't buy?'

'I didn't think that you knew there *were* any,' said Jessica instantly, then regretted her flippancy when she saw the impatient look he gave her. 'If you mean love, I'm sure that they'll give all they have to give.' In Kristin's case, she wasn't sure how much that was.

'Not love ... kindness,' Matt surprised her by saying. 'That's the most valuable gift of all for a child. You know, the children of the wealthy often don't see very much of their parents, they're brought up by nannies and governesses and servants and instructors, whose kindnesses are to a large extent quite impersonal. They aren't given the chance to learn their own value, to touch reality. Freud has it that the capacity to love and the capacity to work are the essences of maturity. It's no wonder that so many rich kids find it hard to relate to other people.'

'Is that what it was like for you? Poor little rich boy?'

He smiled at her acerbic remark. 'No, not really, at least not my early boyhood. My parents had a lot of common sense. But I saw a lot of it at school—children swamped by privilege, arrogant in their uncertainties and suspicious of any friendships. Because they felt secretly guilty of their unearned wealth, and lacked a knowledge of their own worth they couldn't believe that people could like them for themselves, rather than for their name, their money.'

'And you?' she asked softly, seeking another glimpse into his shuttered life.

'I wasn't suspicious *enough*.' His face took on an angular bleakness. 'One of the trustees of my father's estate, a friend—I used to spend the holidays with his family—secretly embezzled hundreds of thousands of dollars from my trust fund. And I wondered why he didn't attend the twenty-fifth birthday celebration they put on for me. He was already in South America.'

'What did you do?' Jessica asked, recognising the echoes of an old rage.

'On *that* occasion, I cut my losses,' he said, with dry emphasis. 'Though I had several contingency plans should he ever come within striking distance.'

'Yes you're very hot on contingency plans,' said Jessica. 'So that explains your paranoia. Well, here's *one* person who's not after your money. You can choke to death on your millions for all I care.'

'No, it's my hide you want, preferably tanned to the wall.'

'Not the wall. I'd make boots out of it and give

myself the pleasure of walking on you all day long.'

'You mean like the geishas in Japanese bathhouses? I might even like it. My spirit could look up from whatever hell you had consigned it to and delight in the sensuous stroke of your souls on my mortal remains.' He was greatly entertained by his own pun.

'Only you could make damnation and death sound erotic,' she said, denying the tingle of her sense.

'I'm a very erotic person, Jess.' As if she didn't know!

'I think we've got off the subject of babies a bit.'

'On the contrary, we're just getting on to it ... all the cute little ways in which they're made.'

'I thought there was only one.' She bit her lip when he laughed outright.

'Your ignorance is showing, dear Amazon. One basic way with a thousand variations. Would you like a demonstration, Love?'

'No!' she snapped, having walked right into that one. 'And don't call me Love.'

He leaned suddenly across the table, letting his eyes wander. 'Can you blame me for having an attack of déjà vu? Same dress, even same perfume! Madame Rochas, isn't it? I went through an entire stock of testers to identify that one.' He saw the shock in her eyes. 'You should know by now, I'm very, very thorough. If I could have tracked you down by scent alone, I would have. I'm surprised you kept that dress, though. That was silly. So was leaving the drink and the flower ... *and* making that phone call. Why, it was almost as if you were *asking* me to come and find you.'

Luckily for her self-possession Kent came back into the room at that very moment, just as she was on the verge of flinging out an angry denial. Had she wanted acknowledgement, recognition of her victory? If so, she had both with a vengeance.

'She's resting,' Kent sighed happily. 'It was just the excitement I guess. She's a bit worried, too, about what's ahead.'

'She needn't be,' said Jessica reassuringly, 'thirty's not old to be having a baby these days. Lots of career women wait until they have established themselves.'

'If you're worried about her, I can give my own doctor a call,' Matt offered.

'No . . . no, she insists she's all right. I'll get the best gynaecologist in Melbourne to come and see her when we get home. But perhaps . . . for tonight . . . Kristin really would like to get some undisturbed rest. Do you think you could put me in the next room?'

'Of course. I'll go and ask Kim to make up the bed.'

All Jessica's suspicions were re-aroused as Matt departed. So Kristin didn't want her husband with her tonight . . .

'You know, I think you're right, this baby might be the making of Kristin,' said Kent, ignoring the fact that Jessica had said no such thing. 'I've always wanted children, but Kristin insisted she wasn't ready. Maybe she's realised that there's a lack in her life. I think that having someone of her very own to love, to be responsible for, and who'll love her without reservation, may be just the thing she needs.'

Jessica didn't think that life was quite that tidy, but she remained silent in the face of Kent's optimism.

When Matt came back Jessica took the opportunity to slip away with a plea of tiredness, pretending not to notice his discreet signals for her to stay. Ducking out of his embrace she fled to her bedroom to repent her flight at leisure. This might be the last evening that they exchanged their teasing banter with its underlying tones of challenge. She doubted whether she'd ever meet another man like Matt, capable of standing up to her in quite the way he did. Thank God, she told herself, as she slid into bed in her underwear and lay staring up at the black rafters overhead. It would be nice to be back fully in control of her life again, wouldn't it? Nice to be out of the emotional jungle she seemed to have blundered into.

Jungles made her think of Kristin . . . a spiteful cat cornered. What would you do, Jessica, if you were a confused neurotic whose selfish desires had been thwarted? She wasn't quite so far gone as to accuse Matt of being the father of her baby, though the suggestion had been there. That little arrow had been aimed at Jessica, but what had she in store for Matt, the object of her desires? One, last, attempt? An all-out effort?

Jessica jerked upright in the bed. *Kristin really would like to get some undisturbed rest.* The hell she would! Had Matt seen the danger? No, the Madonna had fooled him too.

She remembered the silent laughter they had shared this night, his compassion for the as yet unborn child. She remembered past turmoils . . . his insults, his flattery, his coldness, his sensuality, his savage temper and his roused passion. She remembered the times she had actively hated him and, more recently, the times she had come close to loving him. Come more than close.

She was overwhelmed by the stunning realisation, the source of all her fierce protectiveness, her jealousy, her confusion. She loved him, this complicated man . . . this enemy. Loved him with a strength and passion that made a mockery of all her preconceptions of love being a tender, romantic voyage of mutual discovery. This sudden, sharp, jolting emotion, almost vicious in its illogical intensity was totally alien, yet her mind and body absorbed it with a kind of instinctive familiarity that made her wonder whether the whole incredible arrival of Matt in her life had been preordained. Was this to be her object lesson in humility? To fall in love with the one man in the world who had every reason to hate her?

It didn't matter. Nothing mattered right now but stopping Kristin. Quickly Jessica threw off her underwear and searched through the drawer for the despised baby doll nightie. She donned it with a resigned half-sob of laughter and climbed back into bed to wait. It seemed an age before Matt entered his room, with a bump and a curse that indicated that he and Kent may have celebrated with yet another bottle of champagne. He didn't bother to turn on his light and Jessica's ears strained in the darkness as a faint rustle came through the gap in the sliding door. Then there was a faint roar . . . his shower. He was getting into the shower, that hard, muscular body being kissed by the steamy drops of water. She imagined getting in there with him, flattening her wet, naked body to his. Her hands clenched the sheets.

Then she heard another faint sound, the shrrring sound of a sliding door somewhere down the hallway. It could be entirely innocent, of course . . . Kent going to bed, Kristin getting a cup of hot milk from the kitchen! In a flash Jessica was out of her bed, humping up the bedclothes and squeezing through the narrow gap into Matt's room. Since the layout was the same as her own room there was no stumbling in the dark. Quickly she found the bed and scuttled beneath the covers. She nearly screamed as the whole room quaked . . . no, not the room—the bed! It was a waterbed. Jessica rolled her eyes in the dark—baby dolls and waterbeds, conniving women and jealous husbands— this whole scene belonged on the stage!

She lay stock still, waiting for the disconcerting movement beneath her to subside. Then she couldn't resist wiggling a little to set it off again . . . it was rather delicious, and terribly comfortable. Distracted by the novelty she almost missed the whisper of another door ... her own. Her heart fluttered in her chest, part excitement, part relief. She had been right. Kristin was sneaking a look at the hump in the bed ... now she would think it safe to advance to go.

Sure enough, a few seconds later, Matt's door slid quietly open and closed again.

'Matt?' The breathy whisper came at the same moment the shower was cut off. 'Matt, darling, are you there?' Kristin floated further into the room, wearing a long, pale negligee that shrieked seduction. Jessica grinned fiercely in the dark.

'What——?' Matt, coming through from the bathroom, stopped dead as he saw Kristin.

'Kristin? What's wrong? Aren't you feeling well?'

Wrong move, Matt, thought Jessica, lying still as a mouse under the brown duvet, as she watched him walk towards the other woman. You shouldn't get within striking distance. Funny how he had recognised her, even though the room was practically pitch dark.

As he approached, Kristin fell forward into his reluctant arms. 'Oh, Matt!' She pushed her body against his and Jessica strained in the dimness to see him push her away. Instead he stood still, his arms half-raised to hold her.

'Are you sick?'

Dumb, Matt, very dumb. Did he think her pregnancy had turned Kristin into a sweet little earth-mother?

'Oh Matt, I can't bear it!' Pale arms locked around him as Kristin's head rested against his chest.

Neither can I! Jessica leaned over and punched the light button by the bed.

'Now, Matt! After all that champagne are you sure you can handle two of us at the same time?' she gurgled huskily, sitting up, the duvet sliding to her waist to reveal her maribou-trimmed charms.

The two on the floor froze in the limelight, an oddly

disparate couple. Kristin was artfully draped and fully made-up, her hair carefully tousled whereas Matt, clad only in a white towel around his waist, had no need of artifice to enhance his masculinity. Quite the reverse. His stunned expression was quickly masked, though the glint in his eye made Jessica hotly aware of his piquant amusement.

'How did you—? You were asleep!' accused Kristin tightly, giving herself away in her fury.

'Nonsense, I've been here all night,' purred Jessica, 'waiting for Matt.'

Instead of letting him go, Kristin clutched Matt's shoulders more tightly, her voice rising. 'Well, Matt's been waiting for me, haven't you, darling? You don't really prefer her, do you? I'm much more beautiful. And you told me that you hated women who tried to act like men.'

'Oh, I'm no man,' murmured Jessica, licking her lips in what she hoped was a voluptuous fashion. 'You can vouch for me on that point, can't you, Matt? He knows I'm every inch a woman.'

Kristin's eyes were like chips of ice while Matt's darkened in further amusement.

'He was mine before he was ever yours,' Kristin hissed. 'Weren't you, Matt? Remember how it was with us? How much fun we had? How we made love all the time? I bet that cow can't make you feel as good as I did.'

Firmly Matt extricated himself from her grip, holding her gently away from him. 'I won't have you talking like that in front of Jess,' he said quietly. With a shock of fierce pleasure Jessica realised that he was being protective of her. 'What we had was a long time ago, Kris. I have Jess now and you have Kent. He loves you and you're going to have his baby. It will be a beautiful baby, as beautiful as its mother. And you'll be happy, I know you will.' He spoke in a soft, measured tone that was aimed at defusing her half-hysterical rage, flattering and reassuring at the same time. Jessica was slightly awed by his tenderness. He had every right to be furiously angry at Kristin, to cruelly reject her. Instead he was showing a gentle understanding, a sensitivity, that surprised Jessica, even though she knew that she had seen glimpses of it before. Awe melted into a loving pain. Such a man could never have harmed Fiona or Maria. He had been relying on his reputation for ruthlessness to panic his wife . . . he would never have made those threats good. Never. Only his threats had worked too well, instead of driving his wife to the bargaining table they had panicked her into action. Jessica could see now why he had been so furious about her interference and she despaired. The barriers that lay between them were insurmountable. How could he ever begin to love someone who had thrust herself as painfully into his life as she had?

'You don't love me any more!' Kristin's cry was the cry of a child begging for attention. Her tears were real now, not the pretty imitations she had shed at dinner. She didn't seem threatening any more, only scared and lonely.

'Kristin, Kristin? Where are you?'

The call came from the hall, along with the heavy tread of Kent's footsteps. Kristin stiffened, her hands clenching and unclenching at her sides. Matt and Jessica exchanged horrified looks.

'I won't let him go, Kristin, no matter what you do or say!' Jessica declared with a low, passionate, intensity. The other woman stared at her uncertainly, seeing grim determination in the glowing brown eyes. 'I mean it! You can ruin your own life, and Kent's, and you can jeopardise your baby's future. But Matt will survive, and I'll survive with him. The only person who will suffer in the end will be you. Don't let the past rule your life, Kristin, think of the future.'

'Kristin?' There was a tap on the door and then Kent looked in, his face pale and set. 'Matt ... Kristin!' He looked at Jessica on the bed and Matt with a towel around his waist. 'What's going on?' His voice sharp with suspicion.

'Nothing.' Matt patted Kristin's shoulder and moved calmly over to sit on the side of the bed. 'Nothing is going on. Kristin felt weepy, that's all, and came to find Jessica. Girl talk.'

Jessica held her breath but Kristin said nothing. Kent, aware of the tension but unable to interpret it, tucked his wife in the curve of his arm, wiping clumsily at her tears.

'Hey, Kristy, you'll have all day tomorrow for girl talk.' He couldn't quite mask the down-beat of relief in his softly chiding tone. 'Come and talk to me for a while. We'll have to start making plans, you know. You're going to be a sensation when we get back to Melbourne—just imagine all the attention we're going to get. And what about all the buying that we're going to have to do? Shall we fly someone over from Paris or New York to design a wardrobe for you? Something spectacular as befits a mother-of-the-year. Give Princess Di a run for her money, eh?' He continued to talk as he drew Kristin out into the hall, a tender grimace on his face as he silently thanked the two who were watching with relief.

Jessica, having got out of one unnerving situation, now found herself square in the middle of another. As she tried to scramble off the bed it dipped and rocked alarmingly, sending her sprawling, tangled in the silken sheets. Matt swivelled, grinning.

'Like the bed?'

'I don't know,' Jessica swore as her foot became further entangled. 'I've never been on one before.

Don't you get seasick?'

'It's waveless.'

'You could have fooled me.' She lay down, intending to slide out sideways but Matt stretched out too, and edged her sharply over so that the sheets on her other side now became caught under her body. She was trapped like a mummy in its wrappings.

'Oh, it still moves, rather enticingly don't you think?' He rolled on his side to face her, so that the movement rocked her body into nudging his. 'Speaking of which, was it pure luck that you chose to come to my bed tonight or was your enticement strictly for Kristin's benefit?'

'Of course it was,' she said sharply, twitching her nose to try and get rid of the clean, slightly soapy fragrance of him. He had shaved, too, she saw out of the corner of her eye, and his thick hair was curling from the dampness of his shower. The long, powerful length of him was infinitely disturbing . . . and all that skin . . . 'I knew she was plotting something, and then I heard her sneaking around out there. I had to act quickly.'

'And instinctively, mmmm?' His hand came up to brush her hair away from her creamy neck while she frowned steadfastly up at the rafters. 'You didn't have to come and get into my bed, though. You could have pretended to have a nightmare, screamed "fire", any number of clever devices. You're a very clever woman, Jessica, and you're used to thinking on your feet. But instead of doing any of those things you chose to come in here, wearing something you know very well turns me on in great chunks, and play a delightfully provocative charade. You can't tell me that was *all* for Kristin's sake, not when that little pulse in your throat is banging away like a bass drum!'

Jessica clapped a hand over her collarbone but he pulled it away and came up to lean over her. 'Now,

Jess, don't go all coy on me. You know me well enough to have guessed how I would react ... you might as well have sent me an engraved invitation to make love to you.'

He lowered his mouth on to hers, kissing her, nibbling at her lips.

'No, Matt——' she said weakly, knowing the truth of every word.

'Yes, Jess——' He continued to kiss her as he wrenched at the binding sheet, almost tearing it as he pulled it off her. He pulled off and discarded his towel and Jessica gasped at the scalding heat of his body against hers. His legs were long and rough against hers, his chest rippling as he drew back to fondle her breasts through the gauzy fabric of her top. He nuzzled them with his face, moistening the tips through the thin covering so that the material became totally transparent, wetly encasing the stiffening buds. She moaned and he laughed huskily. 'Now do you see the erotic potentialities, lover? Feels good, doesn't it?' His hand was massaging the whispery-soft maribou against her belly, sliding down to cup the lacy g-string, fingers softly questing ... moving, flexing ...

The bed undulated softly, slowly, shifting their bodies pleasurably against each other. Jessica, floating on a sea of sensation, was awash with love. He was so beautiful, so gentle, so exquisitely *slow* ... Dreamily she let him peel off her flimsy garments, the movements beneath her and above her merging into a delicious muddle of hedonistic delight.

'You are so beautiful,' he murmured thickly as he gathered her naked breasts into his hands to admire their smooth warmth and trace the blue veins up the taut slopes to the centres of pleasure.

'Oh, Matt, yes ...' Jessica felt the soft rippling warmth of his tongue, his mouth, as it slid over her body. His fingers stroked and kneaded as he tasted her body, moving over her tender flesh, brushing her thighs, grazing against the throbbing sweetness that nestled between their silken rise. She closed her eyes, feeling the taut expectancy that stretched between their arching, sliding, shifting bodies, stricken by a suddenly greedy urgency that had her rubbing her breasts against him, reaching for bone and muscle, finding his soft-tipped hardness with a glorious thrill of discovery.

She felt him brace himself above her, his knee sinking down between hers. She wanted him with an excruciating need, wanted to feel him sink inside her, wanted him to find pleasure with her and only her. Yet some inner core resisted the idea of allowing a man such complete knowledge of her, even the man she loved. As he moved upon her she put a panicky hand against his chest, fear overriding her body's natural responses. She loved him with every fibre of her being yet she couldn't stop fighting against the ultimate surrender. She gave a panting moan.

He took her wrist and pulled it with gentle firmness over her head.

'No——' she choked, struggling against extortionate desire.

He took her other hand and held it against himself, shuddering at her touch, his voice raw and hungry, barely restrained.

'I'm vulnerable too, Jess. Please, don't fight this. Let it go, Jess, let it go. It's the way it has to be between a man and a woman. Don't be frightened. Its an invasion, but a sweet, sweet invasion, you'll see. And the victory will belong to you as much as to me.'

The words flowed like thick honey over her, his groaning plea wiping away everything but the craving to bind him to her, to ease the painful tightness that racked their bodies. She arched to accept him, the single, powerful, controlled thrust that filled her with strange exultation. And then, while her body was adjusting to a new explosion of sensation, a second and third thrust that buried him deeper and deeper, that reached into her very essence.

With love she accepted him, fuelled his convulsive urgency with her generous ardency, held him, yielded to him, entrapped him in her silken warmth. Lost in the incredible joy of the moment Jessica acknowledged the triumphant, conquering hero. He pushed her body to its sensual limits, made her redefine them and pushed her again. Hung her over the side of the world until, with a final cry she tumbled off with a violence that took them both by surprise, and tumbled him with her, to a groaning fulfillment that had him trembling in her tightly locked arms, a hostage to *her* victory.

CHAPTER TEN

THE jolting and juddering increased and Jessica desperately tried to quell her rising nausea. Pleased that she had managed to get a window seat, Jessica now wondered in horror whether she was going to have to use the brown paper bag tucked into the seat pocket in front of her. She couldn't very well scramble, retching, over the florid-faced man busily feeding his face next to her.

She groaned silently as she closed her eyes. The plane hit another air pocket and she felt the sweat bead her forehead. This was without doubt the worst trip she had ever made, and she couldn't help contrasting it to the first class journey she had made a few weeks ago. Of course, then she had had anger and contempt to bolster her spirits. At this moment she was too weary to be angry and the only contempt she harboured was for herself. She had invited herself into his bed and then acted with shameless abandon.

Jessica bit her lip savagely. Her body still ached with an unaccustomed soreness. Yet it wasn't an unpleasant ache and the sweetness of it mocked her. It made her different. Her body wasn't quite her own any more. Part of it belonged to *him*.

She had been shocked and embarrassed to be woken by Kim. Alone in the wide bed she had blushed at Kim's cheeky grin, and close on the heels of the blush had come the classical virgin recoil. My God, what had she done! What had she revealed by her actions? How Matt must be exalting at her ignominious downfall. While she had slept on he had got up, dressed, and gone out to sign his all-important deal, confident no doubt that she would be submissively waiting for him when he got back, relegated to the place where all women belonged.

Lying there in his silken sheets another thought had hit her with the force of a sledgehammer. They hadn't taken even the most elementary precautions . . . at this very moment she might be pregnant! Jessica was appalled that a woman of her age and intelligence could be so blinded by love and passion that she ignored the consequences of her actions. A baby! What a complication *that* would be.

Finding out from Kim that both the Farrows had gone into the city with Matt, Jessica sprang out of bed to briskly shower and dress avoiding the sight of her own body in the mirror and refusing to give in to the urge to explore herself for differences. Physically she might be changed, but mentally she remained the same, she *must* remain the same. She loved him but he didn't love her and not for the world would she hang around and behave with the pitiful weakness of another Kristin. And if she stayed what would it gain her . . . a few weeks, a few months of his company? The slow death of her dignity and self-respect?

True he had wanted her, but he had got what he wanted . . . over and over again, in one long, glorious, exquisite night. As she packed her bags Jessica felt that her surrender must have lessened her in his eyes, made her no different from any of the other women he had been to bed with. By fighting him she had gained his respect, had made herself unique. It was love that had made her weak, had sapped her willpower. If she stayed she would be defenceless against him. Love and passion had combined within her to become a new, and overwhelming force. She didn't know how to handle it, how to control it and most frightening of all she wasn't sure that she *wanted* to control it.

So she had fled, like a coward.

It had been surprisingly easy. She had hunted through his drawers and found her passport and rung the airport to waitlist herself on an afternoon flight to Auckland.

Kim had passed on a message from Matt that he wanted Jessica to meet the other three in town for lunch after the press conference scheduled for eleven. All Jessica had had to do was to hide her suitcases outside the front door and wait for the taxi that David called.

The flight was three hours of absolute misery. She arrived back at the flat a physical and mental wreck, thankful for a few hours to pull herself together before Jill arrived home. Her partner was surprised to see her, but not unduly so.

Jessica managed to fend off most of her curiosity about Matt by distracting her with amusing accounts of what she had eaten and where she had gone, of the shopping and the sightseeing. But she had been forced to admit, in answer to Jill's sly question about the case she had packed, that, yes, there had been more socialising than expected, and, yes, Matthew Grieve was good-looking, forceful, charming . . . but probably hell to live with for more than a few weeks! Jill had news of her own in return.

'I'm glad you had a good time; no wonder you're looking so fagged. Incidentally, we hardly noticed you'd gone, business has been so good! And hey, remember that New Guinea engineer?'

'Yes?' said Jessica warily, wishing Jill wasn't quite so fond of cliff-hanger conversations.

'Well, we didn't hear another peep out of him, but we *did* hear from his office.' She paused dramatically. 'It's been taken over by guess who . . . one of Mr Grieve's companies—a property development firm.'

'What a coincidence,' said Jessica wryly.

'Isn't it,' said Jill cheerfully as she peeled some vegetables. 'There's a guy called Stevenson in charge, we sent him two secretaries and a receptionist. And we've had queries from a couple of other Grieve companies. Your Mr Grieve is a man of his word.'

Oh yes, an honourable man all round. Jessica changed the subject abruptly, but talking about other things didn't stop her thinking about Matt and thinking about Matt led her to thinking about the night she had just spent in his arms. Their passion had renewed itself endlessly, each satiation exquisitely temporary. *You're so beautiful I can't get enough of you* he had murmured against her skin and proved it by reaching for her again and again in the night—teasing, touching, stroking, holding, scaling the heights with her. One night. A few precious hours. Even as she regretted them she couldn't stop her senses stirring at the memory, her heart squeezing painfully in her chest.

Determinedly Jessica threw herself back into the reassurance of daily routine, and as the days stretched gradually into a week Jessica congratulated herself on her narrow escape. There was nothing from Matt but a resounding silence, proof if she had needed it that he had been relieved by her disappearance. She had been a challenge, that's all. She would never know whether her going had caused him any regrets, had caused any ripples in his life. Probably not. And whatever his explanation to the Farrows, Kristin would have been delighted.

She was annoyed with herself, however, that she wasn't completely the woman she had been before she went away. Her ability to relax had deserted her, and that in turn affected her concentration. Jitteriness became short-temper, impatience became intolerance. She didn't realise the obviousness of her raw feelings until one morning pleasant-natured Kay actually cut her off on the intercom in mid-snarl about a minor hitch in paperwork.

Two minutes later Jill was there, a one-woman deputation.

'Are you going to tell me about it, or do we have to play twenty questions?'

'Tell you what?' snapped Jessica tiredly. She was always tired these days, and proved that she wasn't by working twice as hard. Eating was a chore, and so was sleeping. Her inability to control the functions that had once been as natural as breathing enraged her, but for once rage was no impetus to action, it merely churned around inside her, feeding on itself, finding an occasional outlet on an innocent bystander.

'Are you pregnant?'

'*No!*' It was torn angrily out of her uncooperative mouth. That had been one load off her mind. 'What on earth gave you that preposterous idea?'

'Don't tell me there wasn't a chance, it's written all over you,' Jill appalled her by saying. She pulled up a chair and sat down on the other side of the desk, her round face sympathetic. 'You're not eating, you're pale enough to be anaemic, you have circles the size of car tyres around your eyes—though the clever make-up job nearly covers them—and you're touchy as hell. What else am I supposed to think?'

'That I'm trying to give up smoking?' said Jessica facetiously. She sighed at the stubborn expression in the grey-green eyes across the desk. Jill didn't often dig her heels in but when she did she could be as tenacious as Jessica herself.

So it all came pouring out. Not the *whole* complex story, but the bit that really mattered . . . about falling for Matt and how, oh yes, he had seemed interested in getting Jessica, and only Jessica, to Sydney with him, but it was only a passing interest. Sex was what he had offered and Jessica had been dumb enough to hope for more. Thankfully Jill made no judgments, offered no advice. The only question she asked was whether Jessica was sure that Matt felt nothing for her and, on being assured that it was so, she merely murmured: 'I wonder, though, whether by running away you didn't leave the whole thing rather unresolved? Were you afraid that if he talked to you he'd persuade you to stay? Did you want to be persuaded regardless of his lack of feelings?'

It was too much. Jessica burst into tears. 'Oh, God, how I hate weepy females,' she moaned.

Jill patted her head. 'Give yourself a break, Jess, you've earned a good cry. Best thing for you.'

'Hasn't helped so far,' she sniffed, thinking of the secret floods her pillow had absorbed.

'I didn't say it would *help*,' said Jill lightly. 'But it won't do any harm. I cried rivers after Morris left . . . but then I was always rather free with my emotions. There's such a thing as too much self-control you know. Why should you feel guilty about feeling miserable? Better than stuffing it inside a pressure cooker and having it blow up on you. And taking it out on Kay, who's been your whipping-boy ever since you came back. Maybe if you'd been a bit more open with your feelings when you were with Matthew things might have been different.'

'Hindsight I *don't* need,' said Jessica, recovering herself damply. 'Have I been that much of a bitch?'

'More,' stated Jill uncompromisingly.

Jessica squared her shoulders. 'You can tell Kay there'll be no more spitting tacks. From now on I'm going to be very mature about this.'

Jill groaned, shaking her red head. 'Why does that make me feel even sorrier for you?'

'Don't pity me, for goodness sake,' said Jessica firmly. She had more than enough for herself. 'I made a mistake and I'm paying for it. But it won't be for ever.'

So sure was she that the shutters had finally been pulled down on that aspect of her life that when the letter arrived the next day she was convinced she was in the midst of one of her jerky, jittery dreams.

It was a long, slim, airmail envelope addressed to Ms Wright. It had a Sydney postmark and was stamped 'personal'. For a long time Jessica stared at it, almost choking on hope.

Trembling, she slit the envelope open and drew out the stiff sheet of paper. For a personal communication it was brief, cold, and as bland as the typeface.

Dear Ms Wright

Thank you for your co-operation during the recent merger negotiations. However, your failure to fulfil completely the terms of our verbal contract negates our agreement regarding payment. I refer, of course, to certain securities in my possession. Under the circumstances I shall retain these as guarantees to ensure your future co-operation on similar assignments.

Yours sincerely,

The signature was indistinguishable, but the letter head wasn't. Jessica's hands began to shake violently as she was swept by a shrieking, howling rage. Every vestige of self-control left her as she tore the offending letter to minute shreds, cursing, wishing that it was Matthew Grieve's stinking, lying, blackmailing body she was tearing limb from limb. She threw the shreds into the wastepaper bin and with a cry of fury followed it up with a kick that sent the bin clattering against the wall.

Kay poked her head around the door and surveyed

the resulting mess. 'What did I do this time?'

'Nothing, nothing,' said Jessica hurriedly, in a choked voice. 'I'm just venting my frustrations.'

Kay grinned sympathetically and indicated the bin. 'Rather it than me. Anything I can do?'

Jessica shook her head and waved her out. When the door closed again she wondered whether she dared throw something else. If she didn't take some action she felt she would explode ... that pressure cooker that Jill had talked about.

That vile man! And she had actually been missing him, wanting him, fancifully imagining that perhaps he was missing her too, missing their delightful clashes, kidding herself that she had meant more to him than just a pawn in another power game.

The swine! He had actually got his secretary to *type* that disgusting letter ... he had probably *dictated* it, taking pleasure in making the threats out loud as well as setting them down in black and white!

Jessica gave another, silent, scream, her hand clenching on the airmail envelope. How could he? After what they had done together? How *could* he? Ohhh, she would like to see him suffer. If he was here, now, in this room she would beat him to a pulp—never mind the book of rules, she would use every dirty trick she knew! Temper raced through her veins and she smiled grimly ... at least he had handed her a cure. What woman could love a man who did this to her? She was very tempted to fly back to Sydney just for the sheer pleasure of punching him on the nose. She positively ached to do something.

She unscrewed the envelope, about to accord it the same treatment she had given the letter, when she noticed there was a thin sheet of paper sticking to the inside. Some fresh insult no doubt. Another threat, perhaps written with his own hand.

But no, the second sheet was also typed, and it wasn't from Matt. Jessica frowned as she worked out what must have happened. This was a file copy that had somehow been accidentally put in with her letter. It was to a Michael Stevenson from someone called Karen. Matt's secretary was a Karen. Jessica's heart began to thump as she re-read the body of the letter, picking up on the vital phrases:

Could you airfreight Mr Grieve's strongbox along with the Dixon contracts on the 17th?

Was that the box Jessica thought it was?

The key to the box is in the safe also.

Yes, it was.

The combination is Matthew's birth date. Once you've opened the safe call the security firm and have them rotate the combination for your own use.

Automatically Jessica checked the calender on her desk. Tomorrow was the 17th. Tomorrow the evidence against her would be leaving the country, the evidence that Matt wanted to keep to 'ensure her future co-operation'. The words burned like acid into her brain. And he had actually had the nerve to sign his letter 'yours sincerely'. Sincere in enmity! Obviously he had regretted showing her any softness, allowing her to glimpse his vulnerabilities. God, she was a fool to have thought that he might have respected her. A fool for having thought that his evasive answers about his threats had meant that they had always been empty ones. That was what he had *wanted* her to think. And she had been so anxious for it to be true that she had lost all sense of proportion.

Her rage gained further momentum. Suddenly that

brandy glass and tape rose before her like spectres, symbols of Matthew's perfidity and her own helpless, stupid infatuation with him. She wanted to dash them out of existence the way she longed to dash Matt's brains out!

All at once it hit her. Her mouth went dry and she felt the stirring of that old, dangerous excitement. She looked at the letter in her hand. Such a coincidence was *begging* to be utilised. Getting rid of the glass and tape might not rid herself of all her problems, but it would certainly satisfy her acute thirst for revenge. My God, Matt would go up in flames!

Insidiously, the thoughts crept up on her. She knew his birth date—she had checked him out in his own *Australian Business Who's Who* and snorted at the length of the entry—she also knew the layout of the office and where the safe was. *And* she had the inside help of three of her girls. And if she was caught? Well, then she would *really* know where Matt stood! Recklessly she made her decision. She had done it once, she could do it again!

Jessica strode into the Cheshire Building as if she owned it, smiling brilliantly at the guard in the lobby. Strength and vitality flowed like honey through her veins. She felt as she had when Matt held her in his arms crooning his song of passion—alive, eager, on the edge of a great discovery—drunk almost, on the knowledge of her daring.

'Hello, Miss Wright,' Tina Martin greeted her cheerfully. On the telephone she had said she was happy to take part in an agency survey of permanently placed staff and seeing her young, open, face Jessica felt a tinge of guilt. She consoled herself with the thought that Matt wouldn't blame anyone but Jessica for what was about to happen.

'Hello, Tina. How's the job going so far?'

'Great. Mr Stevenson's really nice—you should meet him.'

'I thought you said he was at a seminar,' said Jessica, a trifle sharply. She had deliberately chosen to come near to five o'clock once she had heard that most of the staff finished at four thirty.

'Oh, he is, but it's only along at the Hyatt. He'll be back at about half past, he just wanted me to wait in case he has any urgent business.'

Jessica spent an anxious fifteen minutes talking to Tina, asking her questions and making incomprehensible notes in a small flip-top pad. She was wondering how to approach a request to look around when Tina took the initiative.

'Look, would you mind if I nipped away and changed? It's just that my boyfriend's picking me up after work and Mr Stevenson might want me to do a few letters. Neil hates to be kept waiting, but he likes me to look nice, you know?'

It was on the tip of Jessica's tongue to say she looked very nice as she was, with her close-cropped blonde hair and modern, layered-look clothes.

'Sure. I'll keep an eye on the phone for you, if you like.'

'Thanks.' Tina whisked out the door with a change of clothes, pausing to give Jessica a huge grin that she returned with startled amusement.

As soon as the young girl was out of sight Jessica slipped into the office that Tina had indicated was now Michael Stevenson's. It was empty, though Jessica checked behind the half-closed door just to make sure. No ogres there today!

It took four, heart-wrenching attempts before she discovered the order in which Matt had combined his birth numbers. As the door swung open Jessica let out a hoarse whistle of relief that changed to shock as she stared at the empty interior. Nothing! What did it mean?

She felt the hairs on the back of her neck begin to prickle. She turned abruptly.

'And I thought I'd broken you of these nasty little criminal impulses of yours, Love. It looks like we'll have to start your re-education all over again.'

CHAPTER ELEVEN

'MATT!' It came out in a horse whisper of disbelief, of mingled hope and fear.

It was a Matthew Grieve she wasn't sure of—a rough, tough-looking stranger. He was wearing faded denim jeans and a well-worn blue linen shirt, open at the neck. A wide leather belt was slung low on the belt-loops at his hips and scuffed tooled-leather boots were on his normally elegantly shod feet. He looked like a cowboy, out-of-place in the sophisticated office, honed to conditioned hardness by a macho lifestyle. And he was oozing silent threat.

'Yes, Matt.' He closed the door behind him and moved into the room to stand astride, arms folded across his chest, black eyes smouldering with a dangerous intensity. 'You didn't think I'd allow anyone else the privilege of catching you red-handed, did you, Jessica?'

'No.' Jessica whispered out loud, not in answer to his question but in denial of the sharp daggers of excitement that were plunging through her.

'Yes.' Again softly, with menace. 'And now you're going to tell me *why*? Why the merry chase? Did you think that you weren't playing sufficiently hard-to-get? Did you think that you had to run away to get my undivided attention?'

'No ... that had nothing to do with it,' she croaked with an effort, fumbling for thought. 'I didn't expect——'

'The hell you didn't!' he swore with violence. 'Don't feed me any tripe about not expecting me to do anything. You knew damned well that I wouldn't let

you go so easily.' He hooked his thumbs over his belt
and shifted his hips forward agressively. 'With you,
running away is the equivalent of an invitation.'

'Are you implying——' she tried haughtily.

'I'm not *implying*, Jess, I'm *telling* you. You know
my motto. When I lose something I want—I don't get
mad, I get even.'

'You get both,' accused Jessica, the first surge of
adrenalin hitting her. He was here. He had come after
her.

'With enough provocation, yes,' he admitted, eyes
narrowing at the way she tossed her head and drew
herself up to his level. 'And let's face it, Jess, you've
been as provocative as hell all the way along the line.'

'Matt ...' She didn't know what to say, how to
begin. How do you tell a man you've known only a few
weeks that you've fallen in love with him? A man who
may very well hate you as much as he desires you?

'Yes, Matt ... the only man capable of making you
leap into the same trap twice.'

'Trap?' repeated Jessica feebly. He was *the only man*
full stop, as far as she was concerned.

'Surely you don't think it's coincidence that I walk
in here while you're in the process of trying to rob me
... yet again.' He abandoned his aggressive stance
and strolled over to casually push the empty safe
closed. Jessica stood her ground frowningly as he
hitched up a leg of his jeans and sat comfortably on
the corner of the desk.

'I ... assumed ...' She hadn't assumed anything.
She hadn't even cared, but to let him know that would
be surrendering to the inevitable before she even knew
what the inevitable was.

'Careless of you. Don't ever *assume* where I'm
concerned, Jess. I planned it, baited it, executed it. It
was almost disappointingly easy.'

Jessica stiffened at the insult and he admired the

way her body lifted in outrage. She was so delightfully proud; it pleased him to see her emerge from her almost trance-like calmness to take fire. His own body's response was automatic.

'Of course,' he continued, lounging mockingly before her, 'I knew you wouldn't fall for it if I gave you time to think. Such fortuitous coincidences rarely occur ... and *never* would any secretary of mine dare to be so careless. You'd soon work that out ... so I put the pressure on. I gave you a time limit. I sent the letter by private mail, making sure that you would get it this morning, and I made you mad enough to throw common sense to the wind. Sure enough, you came raging over here thirsting to draw blood.'

It came upon Jessica like a blinding flash, searing away everything but the memory of the morning's raging despair when she had opened that envelope and had her worst fears confirmed. As if she hadn't been suffering enough, he had actually planned to cause her maximum hurt!

'That rotten, beastly letter,' she choked out. 'You knew I'd think you were serious. You knew I'd feel——' she shut her mouth like a trap.

'What? Betrayed? Funny, that's just how I felt when I found you'd gone,' he said softly. 'Oh ye of little faith. I thought you'd decided to trust me, Jess ... I thought you'd figured out it was all hot air. Do you really think that I could be such a bastard?'

'Yes!' She clenched her fists to stop herself hitting him. Damn him, now he was trying to make *her* feel guilty for her doubts, when he was the one who had deliberately fostered them for his own ends.

'Not true. I'm completely legitimate,' he taunted, 'which is more than I can say for some of your activities.'

'I never would have committed any crimes at all if it wasn't for you!' she flung at him furiously, hiding the pain, the uncertainty, under a reassuring cloak of rage.

Unforgivably he laughed and struck his hand over his heart. ' 'Tweren't my fault, your Honour, my man he done me wrong.'

'You are *not* my man!' she sobbed. At this moment she wouldn't have had him for all the tea in China.

'No? I was once. And not just once . . . how many times was it, Jess? Three? . . . five?'

'Shut *up*!'

'My God, you're beautiful when you're angry. Don't you like to remember how it was when we made love . . . how sweet and soft and meltingly feminine you were, Amazon?'

'I said *shut up*! Or I'll——'

'You'll what? Hit me?' He rose to his feet and he was close . . . too close. His dark brows arched, his face was electric with a fierce, flaring excitement as if he drew sustenance from her fury, as if it aroused him. Jessica could feel the waves of sensual, sexual tension foaming up between them, whipping her body with soft, stinging strokes.

'Come to think of it, I haven't had a good fight since you left. How about it, Jess—are you game?'

Jessica almost buckled at the knees at the invitation in his eyes, in every line of the hard body a hand's width away from hers.

'Shouldn't you be calling the police?'

'What, and spoil my fun? Where's your sense of romance?'

'I don't see anything in the least romantic about this situation,' Jessica lied furiously. 'I suppose that's how you got Tina to play along with this . . . this underhanded trick . . . like that taxi driver. Well, I am not in the least romantic.'

He gave a shout of laughter, the narrow face breaking up into attractive lines. He surveyed her with fond humour. 'You actually believe that, don't you? My darling, you are the most romantic woman I've ever met.' She swallowed at the casual sweetness of the endearment. 'You fight tooth and nail for what you believe in, you're loyal to the point of death ... and you kept yourself beautifully chaste in an unchaste world. If ever a woman was created in the image of romance, it's you.'

'You don't get around me like that, Matthew Grieve,' she vowed, shaking the loose tresses away from her neck. She wished now she had worn her hair up today, but that was another thing that Matt had changed about her. She had a new appreciation of her woman's body, the way it moved, the way her clothes felt against her skin, the way her hair swung against her throat as she turned her head. Her body was no longer an efficient biological machine, it had passion, a heart, a soul.

'No ... words alone aren't good enough for you, nor actions. It has to be both, doesn't it, Jess? Simultaneously. That's the way it is with you, all or nothing.'

'What's wrong with that?' she demanded. 'Why the hell should I settle for anything less? Why should I lie down and lick your feet like a dog just because you petted me once?'

'Bitch,' he corrected in a flat voice that made it a double-entendre. His dark eyes were fixed on Jessica's evasive expression. 'But it wasn't just that, was it? You didn't run away from something that easily resolved ... without even saying goodbye.'

'You didn't seem to want to talk,' she snapped and flushed painfully at his enlightened gleam.

'I overslept, and you looked so beautifully peaceful in my arms. I didn't have the heart to disturb you. And I went off quite certain that what we had shared was rather special, and that we'd see each other at lunch. I should have taken into account that it was your first time, and that you might need reassurance. I would have given you all you needed that afternoon. I was planning to play hooky with you.'

Oh God! Jessica caught the faint scent of sandalwood across the small space between them and her bones went weak. For endless dark hours her senses had been filled with the scent and taste of him. She wanted to reach out a hand and slide it under his open collar, feel his strength, lean against it.

'As it was, when you didn't turn up for lunch or dinner, I had to invent a sick aunt for the Farrow's benefit.'

'Rather mundane, for you,' she sniped weakly, trying to stop herself swaying towards him. She was thoroughly confused now. Why had he come; to make her his mistress? Why, then, didn't he just take her in his arms and kiss her, surely he must know by now that she wouldn't resist, her body language must be fairly screaming it at him!

'I was in a thoroughly mundane frame of mind, I assure you,' he said drily. He moved and every nerve in Jessica's body tingled, but he was backing away to re-seat himself on the desk corner, raising a narrow boot to place it on the chair to Jessica's right. He studied the scuffed tip of his boot in silence, then looked up to catch her staring at the long, muscled extension of his leg. He made a soft sound through pursed lips and shifted his gaze to her legs, outlined by the narrow grey flannel skirt.

'I used to have incredible fantasies about you . . . after that first time we met,' he startled her by saying in a casual, musing tone of voice. The black eyes with their narrow rim of dark chocolate moved up to study the rapid rise and fall of her breasts under the soft georgette blouse. It had been too warm for a jacket but now Jessica wished frantically for its thick barrier. Her breasts tightened painfully against the restriction of her thin, seamless bra, and she was sure that those all-seeing eyes were aware of it. 'I used to imagine you raging helplessly at me, and just as helplessly crying out with pleasure when I came to you. I would never give you your freedom, not until you no longer wanted it. *Then* I would let you go and listen to you beg for my favours.'

Jessica trembled at the erotic intensity of his gaze, his smooth, soft words. And while her body acquiesced, pain formed a tight, hard fist of misery inside her. It was just as she had feared. Everything he felt about her was bound up in the past, fettered by those first few moments when she had ground his pride into the dust and devastated his plans. He only wanted to dominate her, not love her, appease his violent desires and then dismiss her. His eyes reached hers, seeing the fear and fascination there, the innocent bewilderment, and she in turn saw a dark and stormy turbulence as he whispered:

'But that was before . . .'

'Before what?' she dared to ask, equally softly.

'Before I grew to . . . know you. Oh, Jess, Jess . . .' it was a reproach, 'don't you think I can distinguish between fantasy and reality? I admit, quite freely, that when you first walked into this room I wanted to commit violence on you. At that party I had only intended to put the fear of God into you. But you got away, *again*, having made a public exhibition of me, *again*. I wanted revenge. So I laid my plans and waited. I was going to put the fear of God *and* hell into you, make you admit everything and turn the screws by telling you just how unnecessary it had all been. From what I knew about you I thought that would be punishment enough.'

Jessica drew breath. 'But then why——'

'You ask me that?' he said incredulously. 'You flung

it all back in my teeth. Proud, self-righteous ... as if you didn't give a damn for any of it. Resistance, challenge, at every turn. I went a little crazy. All I knew was that I wanted something from you, I'm not even sure that I knew what it was, only that you weren't giving it to me. Like ... drinking salt water when you have a thirst ... it makes you crave more. So I had the brilliant idea of taking you with me until I could satisfy my craving.'

'But ... what about the jewellery ...' husked Jessica, stunned by his confession.

'Aahh ... I made it up,' he said blandly. 'Even I draw the line at being quite that calculating. But you had no trouble in believing it. I was such a villain anything was possible.' He smiled ruefully. 'That's twice I relied on my wicked reputation to do my dirty work for me, and twice it has backfired in my face.'

Jessica stared at him, entirely lost, and he sighed. 'I suppose before we go any further ... we must rid ourselves of all the excess baggage we've been hauling around, at great cost to our relationship.' He leaned back across the desk and shoved open a drawer. He drew out a cassette tape with Jessica's name inscribed boldly on it. and handed it to her. Next he took out the familiar perspex cube and regarded it with a faint, sentimental regret before shattering it, and its contents, with cool precision against the sharp edge of the desk.

The blood roared in Jessica's head. His words, his actions, flowed together in her mind like molten metal ... forming and reforming into incredible shapes.

'They were useless anyway,' he said slowly, watching the flush cross her face as she tried to adjust to a whole new world of possibilities. 'They could never have got back what you stole from me.'

Jessica's head jerked. 'I burned them, the letters ... in your grate.'

'Destroying the evidence; clever Jessica,' he said. The moment was filled with more exquisite, painful delight than any other in his life. The instant before the fall; the relinquishment of the safety line. If he was wrong about her, there was nothing left but the long plunge into darkness. 'But that wasn't all that you stole. It's the other that you must pay for . . . and the prosecution wants a life sentence.'

Jessica shook her head helplessly. 'I didn't take anything else.'

'My heart, Jessica.' The darkness was rushing up at him, but he smiled. She would catch him . . . in her tender, passionately strong grip. She would catch him. 'Isn't that what you said you were there to steal? My heart.'

'No.' She closed her eyes, the word a whispered thread of sound. He knew. He knew that she loved him and he was cruelly teasing her. He didn't need the evidence now, he knew that he could cause her the deepest wound with the merest word.

'Yes. Oh, you didn't succeed right away . . .' He lifted a hand to brush along the prominent line of her cheekbone, finding it damp. 'But later, bit by bit, every piece, Love. Wasn't it obvious? I thought it was, that's why I was such a swine sometimes, I felt so exposed.'

She slid into his arms and he kissed her.

'"a kiss, Long as my exile, sweet as my revenge",' he whispered ravishingly against her mouth. 'You have your revenge, too, Love . . . *my* submission.'

Jessica sank into the kiss, sucked instantly into a whirling vortex of passion, a fire-storm of pleasure made more intense by the strain of what had gone before. Her mouth opened like a flower to the fierce heat of his tongue and the steely soft probe flickered experimentally before thrusting deep for the honeyed sweetness offered him.

His arms came up around her, crushing against his full length her lithe, strong body. She clutched at the broad hardness of his belt as their legs meshed and the violence of that first kiss melted into pure voluptuary. Jessica arched to push her breasts against his muscled chest, twisting her body against him so that he moaned and slid a hand down to still the thrusting movement of her buttocks.

'Oh, God,' he groaned in her ear, biting softly at her neck. 'How could you ever have thought that one night would satisfy me ... a thousand and one wouldn't be enough. I had to come after you.' He kissed her again, asking savagely: 'How in the hell could you have run away from *this*?'

'I had to ... I couldn't stay ... I panicked,' she murmured, hardly aware of what she was saying. 'I was afraid that you would see ...'

'That you loved me?'

She pulled her head back but he wouldn't let her go, his crushing grip tightening as if he would never let her go. He *had* known, he had taken her love and said nothing.

'You knew?' Her eyes shimmered with hurt.

'I wasn't certain,' he told her, his face dark with passion and a fierce tenderness. He bent and rasped the side of his face against hers, a nuzzling, comforting gesture. 'A woman like you, with your strength and ideals, doesn't separate sex from the rest of her being ... you would never have made love with me if you hadn't been emotionally involved. And you were so wild in my arms, almost frenzied with eagerness, and so innocently open in your enjoyment.' His words kindled a blush and when he drew back she avoided his eyes so that he laughed softly, and continued: 'I thought, my God, perhaps there's hope that she's secretly crazy about me ... and I loved you all the more. And then, when you did your disappearing act, for a few seconds after finding out I was actually ecstatic. Nothing, *nothing* could make a coward of my darling Amazon but the realisation of her own vulnerability. And the only way you could be vulnerable was through love. If it was only sex, and you didn't give a damn about me, you wouldn't have turned a hair—not my fearless Jessica.'

'If you knew then why didn't you call me? Why did you wait so long? I thought you had . . .' Her voice broke on the rack of memory. The time they had lost! So many precious seconds, hours, days when they could have been loving each other.

He dropped one arm and tugged her over to the long couch against one wall. It was covered in soft green dralon that sank deeply beneath their combined weight. He turned her so that their bodies were tilted to face each other.

'Because I have just as much pride as you, if not more, and just as healthy a temper. After a few seconds of ecstasy at your flight, I was bloody furious. You had no trust in me at all, did you . . . you turned a loving experience into a one-night stand simply because you didn't trust me.'

'You hadn't given me very much reason *to* trust you,' Jessica felt constrained to point out. 'From the very start you set out to create as much fear as you could. You can't blame me for thinking that you might have carried the fight over into the bedroom.'

Matt put his hands on her shoulders, massaging the bones with his thumbs. Jessica longed to unbutton his straining shirt and bare his chest, to rediscover the hidden delights of his body. He had been such a wonderful lover, so unselfish until the drive to complete his own satisfaction had taken over.

'Jessica?' He shook her slightly so that she blinked and looked up from the tantalising ripples beneath the shirt. 'You knew that by then any threats I made were ringing slightly hollow. I'll admit that at first I meant every word I said. At the time I thought forcing you into going to Sydney with me was a brilliant way to make you suffer for your sins ... to draw out my victory at leisure. But it didn't quite work out like that. My lust for revenge very soon turned into a very different kind of lust, and I discovered that I liked your pride, your obstinacy, that I enjoyed testing myself against the resilience of your mind and body. You must have sensed that, have realised that by the time we made love that I had lost all desire to crush your magnificent spirit.'

'I *wanted* to think that . . .' Jessica couldn't stop her fingers going up to toy with the buttons on his shirt, her other hand moving absently on the flex of his knee. Matt gave a half-sign, half-groan.

'But you didn't trust me . . . perhaps you were right. God knows what confusion we might have created if you had stayed and we had both been afraid to speak. As it was your going made me think, made me sort out my priorities...and you came out top. I was damned if I was going to let you slip out of my life for the sake of pride.'

'But why did you have to go through all this . . .?' Jessica shrugged to indicate the office, not wanting to take her hands off him and buttons sliding inadvertantly out of their buttonholes.

His hands moved down her arms, stilling her fingers. His mouth was curled in sensuous mockery. 'I'm afraid that your advent into my life has awakened instincts I never knew I had. I have this incredible compulsion to crawl under your velvet skin and make you feel everything from the inside out, for *me*.' Jessica closed her eyes and shivered at the insidious pleasure his words invoked. 'You're at your most impregnable when you're prepared. I wanted to unprepare you. You're far more likely to tell me the truth when I take you by surprise, when I enrage and disconcert you. And, I must admit, I wanted to punish you a little for the agonies you've put me through.'

Jessica felt faint at the look in his eyes, the expression of deep, abiding need. It made him look slightly lost and uncertain . . . the way she felt.

'I love you,' she said, and his hands trembled on hers.

'And I love you. If anything convinces me that what I felt for Lisa was merely infatuation it's the way that I feel now. I allowed her the rope to hang herself because I didn't care, and nearly hung myself in the process. Love, companionship, sex . . . they were inessentials then. I was young, ambitious—I should never have married anyone at that stage of my life, let alone Lisa.'

'You mean it's now expedient for you to fall in love?' said Jessica quietly, slow pain stirring.

'I mean that emotionally I was immature, I thought emotion was something one could . . . control. I know better now. I *feel* more deeply than I ever have before in my life, or perhaps it's just because that through you I can free my feelings. I'm no longer afraid of admitting that you can hurt me . . . quite unbearably . . . if you choose. I lay my life in your hands.' He drew her soft palms back against his chest. 'Will you marry me? I know my track record is no recommendation——'

She stopped him with a tender murmur. 'If you had offered me anything less I would have killed you,' she threatened, adding with teasing exultancy: 'Or blackmailed you into proposing. I would have lifted your fingerprints from my body and planted them somewhere compromising. Someone told me that they've invented a laser that can uncover "invisible" prints from *anywhere*.'

His tension vanished and lecherous mockery glinted

in the dark eyes. 'The only person who will be dusting you for prints from now on is me. And I can't think of any place more compromising to plant my fingerprints than on your body. Some of them are in extremely . . . inaccessible positions . . . even for a laser.' He had begun to unbutton her blouse, and she trembled with desire as his fumbling fingers brushed the upper curves of her breasts.

'In fact . . .' he peeled off her blouse and shrugged out of his shirt '. . . it might be a good idea if I went over you and . . .' he felt the soft, moist rasp of his tongue over the sprinkle of freckles in the hollow between her breasts, '. . . wiped off . . .' he ran his tongue over the curve where lace met naked skin, '. . . every single piece of you I ever touched . . .' His hands slid up her bare back and unclipped her bra then snaked down to find the zip of her skirt.

Jessica gasped, half-laughing. 'But you're not wearing gloves, you're making even more.'

He dispensed with her skirt and slip. 'I know,' he growled huskily, 'I'll have to do it all over again . . . and again.' His mouth dipped, moistened, nibbled and moved on until Jessica was beyond appreciating the joke. She moaned and sighed and twisted and turned under the roving mouth, the dabbling fingers. She was lying full length on the couch and he on top of her, the swollen evidence of his desire clearly outlined against her thighs, even through the harsh denim of his jeans. She lifted her hips as he parted her legs, pressing herself against him to assuage some of the burning ache. Then she opened her eyes . . . and choked.

'Matt!' He didn't stop his soft, implacable explorations, he merely groaned as she stiffened beneath him, creating new pressure points. 'Matt. *Matt!*' she wailed, trying to tug his head away from the silky flesh of her breasts by the thick, dark hair. 'There's a security camera up there!'

The single, cool, grey, malevolent, all-seeing eye was staring at them from above the door.

He bit the succulent tip of her breast and feathered a caress against her inner thigh. 'Didn't you ever want to be in the movies?'

'Not blue movies!' cried Jessica, appalled at his disinterest as much as she was flattered that she could arouse him so much he would make love to her practically in public. 'Matt, *please*.'

He relented and placed a soothing kiss on her navel, a hand preventing her from frantically covering her breasts. 'Don't hide them, I love your breasts, they're practically the first thing I noticed about you. The camera's not connected yet ... the system was only installed today.'

'You might have said ...' Jessica protested weakly, welcoming the return of his full weight on top of her. Her hands slid over the smooth mucles of his back, her fingers digging in in tender chastisement. He responded with a satisfying arch of his back that thrust him closer between her legs.

'Why, I like it when you get frantic ... and don't worry about the door either ... this time I *did* lock it after us.'

'You are a very devious man,' Jessica sighed with pleasure.

'Mmmm, and I'm rapidly learning to be even more devious. Here ...' He braced himself on one arm and twisted his hips sideways, drawing her hand down to his buckle. '... Show me some more of your celebrated breaking and entering.'

'I never did that,' breathed Jessica, her hands shaking as she helped him unzip his jeans and slide out of his clothing. The flat hardness of his stomach, the flaring hips and powerful nakedness of his thighs made her whole body tauten with delicious anticipation. 'I ... it was only ever trespass.'

'Then trespass some more,' he urged as he dealt with her tiny lace panties and brought their bodies together with deliberate slowness. The solid, jutting masculine angles fascinated Jessica and she delighted in Matt's groan as she obeyed his plea. 'Trespass all you like ... you have a life sentence to fill—starting now!'

Harlequin Presents

Coming Next Month

Available in June wherever paperback books are sold, or through Harlequin Reader Service.

In the U.S.
901 Fuhrmann Blvd.
P.O. Box 1397
Buffalo, N.Y. 14240-1397

In Canada
P.O. Box 2800, Postal Station A
5170 Yonge Street
Willowdale, Ontario M2N 6J3

Can you keep a secret?

You can keep this one plus 4 free novels

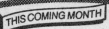

Harlequin Intrigue

WHAT READERS SAY ABOUT HARLEQUIN INTRIGUE . . .

Fantastic! I am looking forward to reading other Intrigue books.

*P.W.O., Anderson, SC

This is the first Harlequin Intrigue I have read . . . I'm hooked.

*C.M., Toledo, OH

I really like the suspense . . . the twists and turns of the plot.

*L.E.L., Minneapolis, MN

I'm really enjoying your Harlequin Intrigue line . . . mystery and suspense mixed with a good love story.

*B.M., Denton, TX

*Names available on request.

WORLDWIDE LIBRARY IS YOUR TICKET TO ROMANCE, ADVENTURE AND EXCITEMENT

Experience it all in these big, bold Bestsellers— Yours exclusively from WORLDWIDE LIBRARY WHILE QUANTITIES LAST

To receive these Bestsellers, complete the order form, detach and send together with your check or money order (include 75¢ postage and handling), payable to WORLDWIDE LIBRARY, to:

In the U.S.
WORLDWIDE LIBRARY
901 Fuhrmann Blvd.
Buffalo, N.Y. 14269

In Canada
WORLDWIDE LIBRARY
P.O. Box 2800, 5170 Yonge Street
Postal Station A, Willowdale, Ontario
M2N 6J3

Quant.	Title	Price
_____	**WILD CONCERTO**, Anne Mather	$2.95
_____	**A VIOLATION**, Charlotte Lamb	$3.50
_____	**SECRETS**, Sheila Holland	$3.50
_____	**SWEET MEMORIES**, LaVyrle Spencer	$3.50
_____	**FLORA**, Anne Weale	$3.50
_____	**SUMMER'S AWAKENING**, Anne Weale	$3.50
_____	**FINGER PRINTS**, Barbara Delinsky	$3.50
_____	**DREAMWEAVER**, Felicia Gallant/Rebecca Flanders	$3.50
_____	**EYE OF THE STORM**, Maura Seger	$3.50
_____	**HIDDEN IN THE FLAME**, Anne Mather	$3.50
_____	**ECHO OF THUNDER**, Maura Seger	$3.95
_____	**DREAM OF DARKNESS**, Jocelyn Haley	$3.95

YOUR ORDER TOTAL	$_____
New York and Arizona residents add appropriate sales tax	$_____
Postage and Handling	$ .75
I enclose	$_____

NAME _____

ADDRESS _____ APT.# _____

CITY _____

STATE/PROV. _____ ZIP/POSTAL CODE _____

WW-1-3

HARLEQUIN BRINGS YOU

Janet Dailey

★ AMERICANA ★

A romantic tour of America with Janet Dailey!

★

Beginning in June, enjoy this collection of your favorite previously published Janet Dailey titles, presented state by state.

Available in June wherever paperback books are sold or reserve your copy by sending your name, address and zip or postal code, along with a check or money order for $2.75 per book (plus 75¢ for postage and handling) payable to Harlequin Reader Service to:

Harlequin Reader Service

In the U.S.
901 Fuhrmann Blvd.
P.O. Box 1397
Buffalo, NY 14240

In Canada
P.O. Box 2800
Postal Station A
5170 Yonge Street
Willowdale, Ont. M2N 6J3

JDA-A-1